I0681944

AMERICAN

Z

J.G. FLETCHER

This book is a work of fiction. Any reference to historical events, names, characters, businesses, organizations, governments, military, places, events, and incidents are either the product of the author's imagination or are used fictitiously. Any resemblance to actual persons, living or dead, events, or locales is entirely coincidental.

Copyright © 2017 by J.G. Fletcher

All rights reserved. Except as permitted under the U.S. Copyright Act of 1976, no part of this publication may be reproduced, distributed, or transmitted in any form or by other means, or stored in a database or retrieval system, without the prior written permission of the publisher or author.

Published by
TSOMBIE Inc.
A Phase III Publishing Company
Clarksville, Tennessee
https://tsombie.com
https://jg-fletcher.com

ISBN: 978-0-692-95473-7

eBook ISBN: 978-0-692-94412-7

Library of Congress Control Number: 2017914748

For my kids

ONE

I'm going to die, Julia says to herself. I'm going to die alone, forgotten. I'm going to die cold, hungry. Focus Julia, she tells herself. If you are going to die, then don't spend the small amount of time you have left being angry. Focus Julia, she keeps repeating to herself in a low, monotone whisper. Think about your brother, focus on the memories with him and relax. Relax Julia, that's it, die a calm death, a calm death of carbon monoxide poisoning, slow and easy. If the air filtration system in the bunker was planned to last as long as the food rations, then my time is up, she thinks. I love you Brian, and I guess I'll be with you soon mom. Hopefully that is heaven, for both of us.

Five bottles of water and two cans of vegetable soup are all that remained left from a year's worth of food in the underground bunker, which Julia's dad had built. Julia stopped counting the days back in September, but she knows that it is sometime in December. The food rations were neatly organized by her father over the years, as he continually built up the bunker for any doomsday scenario that might occur. Asteroid strike, nuclear fallout, you name it and it appeared as if he was prepared for it with this bunker.

Julia's father spent the better part of his life devoted to the military and was usually gone during the important times of a young girl's life, those times when they all need a father. Julia always reminded him of this as she grew older and into a young, independent woman.

Now as the air filtration system slowly sputtered into broken gaps of silence, she wanted to remind her father once again that he was not around, once again when she needed him. This was his bunker though. That fact kept clawing at Julia's curiosity. Why would he leave as soon as a disaster happened? What would be the point of preparing for so long to save your daughter from a disaster, if you aren't even going to be there with her?

Julia tries to stop thinking about her dad, but it is useless. What happened? Julia begins another conversation with herself. Over the past year she had learned to be the optimist and pessimist, the fun and the boring, her own yin and yang. It was one of the few things that helped her keep her sanity. She enjoyed most conversations with herself, and sometimes she would even pretend to be other people, like Brian, her old friends, and sometimes even her dad. When she first began having these lengthy conversations with herself, she thought she was losing it and began to panic. But then she relaxed when she grasped the concept that it didn't matter, it wasn't like anyone knew, or would ever know for that matter.

I hate not knowing what happened out there, she continues her conversation. Had a huge natural disaster really occurred? Was Brian okay? Was there a nuclear war? Maybe North Korea really succeeded? Every day for the past year, she had been imagining what happened, dwelling on why her father put her down there.

Really Julia! She barks loudly, as she takes on a different personality within her own conversation. Are you really still believing your father right now, still believing that something happened? Nothing happened Julia. I can't believe you're still buying into his crap when you're about to die. There was nothing major on the news that was going on, no disaster or imminent war. Maybe he finally snapped, because he accepted the fact that there was no end-of-the-world disaster coming? Maybe he couldn't face the fact that he had wasted his whole life, preparing for something that was never going to happen? And he just couldn't bear to tell me how embarrassed he was, and that he was wrong, for once.

I can't believe that he would actually let me die down here though, rather than tell me he was just a paranoid, crazy, old war-veteran. I mean, I knew the man was weird, but I never thought that his paranoia would get the best of him. And I never would have imagined that it would ultimately lead to me dying, here in this bunker, alone and forgotten.

What was that? Julia gasps to herself. Was that the wall? Okay, I know that hallucinating is a side effect of carbon monoxide poisoning, but it sounded like a safe or something just opened, and I swear that wall just moved. Whoa! What the? The floor just moved!

"Wait for the opening…" Those were the last words he said to me when he shoved me down here last year. Well this is definitely an opening. Thanks for clarifying dad. Maybe I won't die in this isolated doomsday bunker after all.

Julia's brief moment of excitement is clouded with anger again, almost immediately. Really Dad! You couldn't have taken ten seconds to just tell me up front that everything would last a year down here? Or tell me that the bunker would unlock one day, and I could leave? She cries for a few seconds and then calms back down.

Well, he never could tell me three words I wanted to hear my whole life. So maybe my expectations are a little high for a complete sentence before I die? She chuckles to herself.

Julia stares with confusion at what she is now looking at, there beneath her feet, in the newly opened floor. Lying in the open were multiple weapons, pistols, rifles, and knives. He must have assumed that if I had access to these in the beginning that I might have already ended it, Julia thinks quietly to herself.

Well I can't take them all, she says out loud. Why the hell did he put so many weapons down here if I was the only one that was going to be here? Julia asks herself, as she paces around. It doesn't make sense. The food was separated in single person rations and I counted an exact year's worth before I opened any of them. And the air filtration stopped when I only had two days of rations left. So why are there enough weapons in this bunker to supply a small village with? Maybe I'm over thinking it? Maybe he just kept them down here for safekeeping, instead of out in the open, instead of back in our house? But what if I am not...did something go wrong? I mean, did he really expect Brian, or some of his war buddies, to be here with me too? There's no way. Brian was all the way on the East Coast, in North Carolina with his father-in-law Trent, and Trent's new wife. So why all the weapons? Sure, he's got his doomsday buddies and veteran friends, but it was months before he put me down here since I last saw them. So why all the weapons? Think simple, Julia tells herself quietly, think simple.

Screw it. He said wait for an opening and the wall opened. Yep, I'm out of here. I'm grabbing what I can carry and then I'm leaving this bunker, finally. I'll take my chances out there because there is nothing more left for me here, nothing except the haunting memories of an abandoned daughter, left alone, left forgotten.

Julia turns on the headlamp and pulls on the edge of the wall that was opened. And she begins walking, just to find a series of walls that are all in close proximity to each other. The walls are all padlocked with the keys taped to the locks. She remembers there were three hatch openings coming down into the bunker, when she was shoved down it over a year ago by her dad. Maybe the walls were designed the same, she thinks, as multiple layered protection from something.

Taped to the third wall is what appears to be a map, with directions highlighted, a compass…and a note?

-Julia,

I'm sorry I couldn't explain all of this to you, I always thought the less you knew growing up then the better chance you had to live a normal life. I know I was probably not the father you wanted growing up, and I'm sorry if I disappointed you throughout your life. But still I look at you, and I can already see myself in you Julia, already at such a young age. I know you probably don't want to hear that right now, at your current age, but we are the same Julia. Anyways, if The Society succeeded with Phase One then I'm guessing that it's pretty close to the year 2019 if you're reading this. It looks weird writing that number down right now, so far away. You are all grown by now, and hopefully you remember the few times I actually spent some quality time with you, and you can remember what I taught you over the years. I am going to need your help now Julia. I will explain more when I talk to you on the phone and finally see you once again in person. I just hope that I have not betrayed your trust so much that you will hate me, hate me as your father, or hate me as the man you have seen me become over the years. Follow the map and then follow the instructions once you get to the safe-house. I will be in touch as soon as I can.

-Dad

Julia thinks for a second after putting the letter down. How would he know that he would still be alive, if he wrote this letter all those years ago, long before putting me down here? Why! Why would you do this to me?

Julia stops thinking about it and begins moving again. She slowly opens the third wall into a long, dark tunnel of nothing. No more walls. She begins walking. Then she stops after just a few steps. Julia holds her breath as she hears the faint sound of helicopter rotors, buzzing faintly overhead, through the tunnel ceiling.

Thank you! She yells out. I knew it, I knew it. He is certifiably insane. I'm going to kill him. I'm literally going to kill him for doing this to me. Helicopters flying around obviously means people are alive. So how bad could it be? She thinks confidently. Okay Julia, let's hoof it. This tunnel can't be that long. Julia shines her headlamp into the cold cloud of darkness in front of her and begins moving again, this time running.

TWO

"Captain Brown, you have a call from Dr. Singer sir." A young man says.

"I've got to send out a few emails Sergeant Jones, tell him that I'll call him back in just a few minutes."

Captain Brown closes his office door and changes out a SIM card on a disposable, prepaid cellular phone.

"Dr. Singer, it's me Justin. Line is secure sir."

"Did you see anything?"

"No sir. There was no marking. Are you sure she…"

"Stop. Don't even think about saying it. I know she's alive okay. We just need to give her a little more time. I know she's okay."

"Sir, I can go back out and search the cabin, or search the area around the exit point of the bunker. But you will have to tell me where it is. She might be lost sir."

"No, we are absolutely not going to do that. And she's not lost anyway, not her. And you know I can't tell you the location of the bunker. There's too much risk involved with that. I told you time and time again, you can't trust anyone Captain Brown. You could be followed and watched at all times."

"Well Dr. Singer, with all due respect, you trust me sir. I mean how do you know everyone in my office, my unit, is not involved in your conspiracy theory? How do you know for sure that I'm not? What if I am one of them? Whoever they are. Why do you trust me?"

"Captain Brown, I told you before that…"

"Don't Captain Brown me okay! I'm tired of all the games and I want some answers sir, now. I can't keep sneaking around like this, lying to everyone in my unit, my friends, my wife. You think you have something on me because I told you what happened while I was deployed? But I don't care about that anymore. I'll deal with those consequences if you expose my skeletons, but can you deal with the consequences if I expose yours? You have basically been blackmailing me over the past year. Having me access hundreds of government files, do all your little secret spy missions, flying around, and then stalking all those people. I want answers and I want them now, or I'm walking."

Captain Brown stops talking and waits for a response. There is silence on the other end of the line. He calms down.

"Look, regardless of how messed up I am, I still had a decent life before I met you. And how do you really know, I mean really know, that I haven't told my wife? Or a neighbor? Or a friend? How do you know I haven't exposed you already? Dr. Singer, how do you know?"

Dr. Singer lights a cigarette and starts smoking. Justin can hear him striking the lighter, then inhaling and exhaling slowly over the phone.

"If you had told someone, you wouldn't be alive right now for one. You wouldn't be having this conversation with me. You want to know everything huh? Well answer me this then, don't you think it's weird that you didn't get sick when the flu season started last year?"

"Now what are you talking about? No, it's not weird. I didn't get the flu. So what? That is kind of what getting the flu shot does you know, keeps you from getting sick. And for crying out loud, what does that have to do with anything?"

"But you have had the flu before, right?

"Yes. And your point is what?

"I can't discuss this over the phone. Look, you're right about deserving to know more, to know the truth about everything. I have kept you in the dark long enough. Schedule your next rehabilitative therapy appointment with my assistant, as normal, and I'll tell you everything when we meet. No more delays. Goodbye Captain Brown."

"Dr. Singer? Hello? Dr. Singer!"

Justin slams the phone on his desk and pushes his chair back against the wall.

"Is everything alright sir?

The young sergeant opens Captain Brown's door and stands at the entrance, looking at him with a blank, unemotional stare.

"I'm fine sergeant. The doctor says my recovery is going a little slower than expected, that's all. I just want to be done with this therapy you know, no worries. Sorry about the commotion. Schedule my monthly appointment with Dr. Singer's assistant please. That'll be all, thanks sergeant."

"Yes sir."

The sergeant turns around and begins to exit the room, closing the door behind him.

"Hey, Sergeant Jones, let me ask you a quick question. I'm just curious, did you get sick last year with that nasty flu virus that was going around?"

"Yes sir. I made a full recovery. Why do you ask sir?"

"No reason in particular. I just remembered that it's about to be that time of year again, that's all. Make sure everyone is up to date on their shots in the unit please."

"Yes sir. That is already taken care of. Our unit is scheduled to get flu shots next week sir."

"Great. I'm about to leave for the day okay. The wife's got dinner waiting on me, spaghetti night, again."

Captain Brown lets out a little grin after his display of fake enthusiasm, but the sergeant doesn't seem to respond.

"Have a good night sir."

THREE

How long is this freaking tunnel? I mean seriously, Julia says to herself in disbelief. Julia slows down to a light jog, then a walking pace. Okay, that's enough cardio, cave girl. You need to take a break. Julia sets down the rifle she is carrying and opens up her bag. Only three bottles of water left, I can't run myself into dehydration. She opens a bottle and takes a slow, but long drink.

Let's see…an average nine-minute mile pace, for over twenty-five minutes…that's at least two and half miles. And that's on top of the thirty minutes I walked before that. Close to five miles, give or take, sounds about right.

Five miles give or take? Are you kidding me right now dad! Julia chucks the bottle of water down the tunnel, about ten yards ahead of her. She hears it echo off something metallic, not stone. She zooms in with her headlamp on where the sound came from and begins to squint with her eyes. Another wall? Come on, really? Irritated, she gets up and walks to another wall and lock. She pauses before she opens it. I swear, if this tunnel keeps going after this. Come on, move. Man, this thing is hard to open. Umph! Julia struggles for a few moments, shifting her weight back and forth, trying to open the wall door.

Got it! Oh, you have got to be kidding me. What is this, a cave? Wait, wait, wait, I think I can see some light. Julia walks slowly to the opening of the cave and is almost blinded by the sunlight. Her eyes have not been accustomed to radiant light for an entire year. She stumbles, and her eyes begin to water as she looks out into the forest, full of trees, and the leaves on the ground. She looks up and into the beautiful, open, blue sky. She falls to her knees and begins to weep softly, clinching the dead leaves and fresh earth with her fists.

Julia pulls the map out of her pocket and wipes the tears from her cheeks. She studies the map and studies the two dots that are annotated in red ink. She thinks for a moment, studying the initials 'SP' beside one, and 'EP' beside the other one. There is also '320' written in black. SP, EP? Start point, end point, Julia thinks. Memories of camping with her father, when she was young, rush to her mind.

- "Okay Julia, our SP is going to be here, where we are now, and our EP is going to be there, at the lake."

"What do the initials mean?"

"Start Point and End Point. Can you remember that Julia?"

"Yeah, Start Point and End Point. But why do we have to use initials, why can't we just say the words?"

"Well, think of it like a code, a code that someone else besides us might not know. And you want to keep that code a secret, so they don't find out. You like keeping secrets, right Julia?"

"Yeah! This is fun daddy!"

"Okay, so then you take the compass and line the degrees up here, like that. And that's how you walk straight to a point. Pretty simple, right? And remember to pick up a pebble, or stick or something, every time you walk a certain distance. That will help you keep track if you go a long way. You remember how many of your steps are in a quarter of a mile right?"

"Yes daddy, I remember." -

Julia wakes from the memory and back to her surroundings, taking in another deep breath of fresh air. She picks up her things and starts her two-mile trek that she had measured out on the map, downhill and through the mountainous terrain.

* * *

Julia bends down and picks up her seventh pebble. She then looks up to what appears to be a small cabin in the distance. She takes a harder look. This is not the cabin she visited as a child with her father, she thinks. This cabin she is looking at now is much smaller, much more primitive. Safe-house, she thinks.

She continues moving forward, toward the cabin. As she gets closer she hears a limb crack in the distance, and she stops dead in her tracks. She draws her rifle up slowly to her shoulder and steadies her aim. She scans with the rifle in a complete circle around her position, and then aims back at the cabin. She walks slowly, with her rifle up and safety off, and ready to open fire, on anyone.

She peeks into the crooked windows but can't really see anything through the thick and somewhat dark curtain hanging down. She creeps around to the front porch and slings her rifle to her side, slowly pulling a small caliber pistol from her backpack. Hammer cocked back, she walks step by step, heel to toe, carefully towards the front door.

Deep breath.

She quickly turns the knob and thrusts the front door open, maintaining steady aim with the pistol the whole time. She quickly scans left, and then right. Nothing. She moves in to look behind the door, nothing there either. Moving room to room, breathing heavy and ready for anyone to jump out, she clears the entire cabin.

After realizing that she is safe, and nobody is there, she puts down her weapons and backpack, and then she starts searching for a phone line. Nothing. She checks the cabinets and kitchen and finds a couple of useful things. A surplus of food, water, non-perishables and a combination locked briefcase. As she picks up the briefcase, she hears the front door creak once, and then again. Then footsteps. She quickly grabs her pistol back off the table and moves behind the kitchen wall. There is a loud clack of wood hitting the floor. Julia holds her breath and begins to tremble, slightly.

"Ahh! Really?" A man's voice says. "I'm getting too old for this."

The man coughs and sits the rest of the wood from his arms down on the floor. He steadies himself back upright and sees the rifle and backpack on the table.

"Julia? It's me, Tommy, Tommy Roark. Julia?"

Julia drops her weapon down with relief at hearing the name and begins to recognize the voice, the familiar voice of Tommy Roark. He was like a part-time father for Julia, when her dad wasn't around for months at a time. But then Julia remembers what her dad's note said, don't trust anyone. She puts a firm grip back around the pistol.

"How do I know I can trust you? What are you doing here Mr. Roark? I'm not sure if you know where I've been for the past year, but let's just say it's been a rough year. And I'm a little paranoid right now. All thanks to you know who. But he never said anything about you being here."

"I know Julia, I know, but let me try to explain here. Your dad, he is alive Julia, and he sent me here. I'm not going to hurt you, I would never do anything to hurt you Julia. You were like a daughter to me. You know that, don't you?"

Julia quickly turns from behind the wall and aims her pistol at his chest, without a hint of hesitation. She notices the rifle slung on his back. She slowly cocks the hammer back on her pistol again.

"Put your rifle down old timer. And do it slowly."

"Okay, okay. I'm putting it down Julia. Be careful, just take it easy."

He begins to take the rifle off his back, slowly, and then kneels down, gently placing it on the ground. He slowly raises back up, using the arm of a chair to brace himself, and then begins to cough. He coughs hard for a few seconds. He pulls a small rag from his jacket and wipes off his mouth. He notices the little splatter of fresh blood, now smeared on top of a previously dried stain.

"I'm just an old, sick man, Julia. I couldn't hurt you if I tried. I don't think I have the energy for that."

Julia slowly de-cocks the hammer and lowers her pistol. But she doesn't put the pistol away, signaling to Mr. Roark that she is not going to shoot him but doesn't fully trust him either.

Mr. Roark takes a hard seat on the couch. Julia looks at him, watching him carefully. He had definitely changed since the last time she seen him. His face was now sunken in, facial bones clearly protruding. His muscular build was obsolete now and his clothes were almost falling off him. But his eyes, his brown eyes were still warm and nonthreatening.

"There's a brief-" He coughs out and stops in mid-sentence.

"There's a briefcase, over there on the table. It's from your dad. He said there's a letter explaining why I'm here, and he said you probably wouldn't trust me until you read that letter. I can't open it. He never gave me the code. He said you would be able to figure it out."

Julia moves backwards to get the briefcase, never breaking eye contact with Mr. Roark. She picks it up and then walks forward, back to the living room. She takes a seat across from Mr. Roark in the chair, facing the couch, watching him. She keeps the pistol in one hand and begins to rotate the number on the first dial of the briefcase, now in her lap. She wonders why her dad wouldn't give him the combination if he trusted him. Then she quickly concludes that it's probably some kind of test or something, a test that her dad planned. She continues rotating the dial.

Mr. Roark watches her gun with a wandering gaze, at the gun and then at her face. He leans his head forward and wipes his mouth with the rag again.

Without really having to think too hard about what the number could be, Julia quickly remembers her dad's pin code system. He taught it to her when she was just a kid and he used it for it everything with a number lock.

Three numbers...first number is always one. She slowly clicks first dial to 1. Then multiply by total numbers needed, three. She clicks second dial to 3. Then multiply by the total number needed again...she clicks the last dial to 9. The brackets pop open and Julia smiles for a brief second.

Mr. Roark exhales a sigh a relief and rests his head on the back of the couch.

Julia's eyes open a little wider. Lying beside the letter are passports, cash, and a couple of cell phones. The passports all have her photo in them, but all with different names, different addresses, and different countries. Questions begin to race through her mind. She quickly pulls the note out and clicks her headlamp on. It was beginning to get dark and there were no lights in the cabin, no signs of electricity.

-Julia

*I hope Tommy is still alive, I hope you didn't hurt him...*Julia glances over at Mr. Roark on the couch, with his head still laid back, and then continues reading...*I know I told you not to trust anyone, but you can trust Tommy. I would have put him in the first letter but I didn't know for sure that he would be able to help back then, and there wasn't enough time for me to go back and change the note. And he is not infected, but he is sick. He has terminal cancer, and probably won't make it through the winter. He will need you to help him, just as you will need his help. I knew a lot about what was going to happen Julia, but I didn't know everything, and I couldn't take any chances with your safety. There are still some unknowns about who is susceptible to being infected and who is immune. I know you don't* *understand what I am talking about and I have a lot that I have to tell you, but I want to tell you in person. There's an orange panel in the bedroom, take it and place it on the roof of the cabin. You cannot make contact with anyone now that you are out in the world again. We are dead Julia. Everyone you knew in your life, my life, believes we are dead, and the only way for us to have a chance is to keep it that way. That includes Brian. I'm sorry Julia, there was just no other way to ensure our safety. Your new primary identity will be Dr. Erica Gordon, a bio-chemist from California. There's a background sheet on each of the identities in the briefcase. I need you to rest and prepare to assume your new identity. I will call you within a week, after the orange panel is placed on the roof and I know you are alive and okay.*

-Dad

Julia lowers the letter and tries to absorb and comprehend everything. Mr. Roark raises his head slowly, coughs, and then stares at Julia, through the darkness in the dimly lit cabin.

"Hello Dr. Gordon."

FOUR

Captain Brown pulls into his driveway and clicks the garage door opener on his sun visor. He parks in the garage and smokes the end-of-day cigarette, before going inside. He is greeted by the familiar Monday night smell of Italian sauce and garlic bread as he walks in the house.

"Let me guess, spaghetti?" He says jokingly to his wife and waits for a response.

His wife doesn't reply to his, somewhat sarcastic, remark. She just continues to stir the pot of noodles over the stove, not reacting at all.

"Hello? Earth to Claire, I'm home."

He taps her on the shoulder and his wife drops the wooden pasta spoon and jumps a little, appearing to suddenly awaken to her husband's presence.

"Hello, Justin. Welcome home. Dinner will be ready soon. I am cooking spaghetti."

"You okay baby? You look like you had one of those weird, spaced out moments again. Everything alright?"

"Yes. I'm fine. I'm sorry, I must have just zoned out for a second. How was your day? Any updates on your therapy?"

"I have my monthly appointment next week and I am supposed to get an update then. Dr. Singer said he...well he said he would tell me at the appointment. Hey, do you remember when you got sick around this time last year, with that nasty flu bug that was going around?"

"Yes. Why do you ask?"

"No reason really. It's about to be flu season again, so I just hope you don't get sick again, that's all."

"Thank you. Do you worry about me? You don't need to worry about me. There's a small staff from the hospital actually coming to our building next week. They are going to administer shots to all of the company's employees."

"You know I worry about you Claire, you're all I've got."

Captain Brown takes off his coat and wraps his arms around his wife, and they begin to kiss each other, gently.

"I think I'll take my desert first tonight," he says softly. They continue to kiss and start moving slowly to the bedroom.

FIVE

"He told you?" Julia asks Mr. Roark in disbelief. "What else did he tell you? What does he mean infected? A virus? What is he talking about? He always made it seem like he was preparing the doomsday bunker for an asteroid strike, or a nuclear attack, or something along those lines. And why didn't you…"

"Just slow down for a second Julia, just calm down. I'll tell you what I know. Here, let me get you a blanket and something to drink. Can you get the fire going? My bones don't work so good in this cold weather."

Mr. Roark pulls a flashlight from his pocket and retrieves a blanket from the closet in the hallway. He drops the blanket off and goes back to the kitchen. The light reflects off the rifle on the kitchen table. He recognizes it as her father's personal rifle, the one he used most often when they hunted deer together. He tears open a new pack of bottled water and walks back to the living room. He sees Julia at the fireplace, glowing softly from the freshly started fire.

"I see you still have your father's taste in weapons. You know I gave him that rifle, I gave it to him…"

"You gave it to him after you got back from Somalia," Julia interrupted. "I know the story Mr. Roark, I've only heard it a thousand times."

Mr. Roark looks at her and smiles, and then lets out a light cough.

"Yeah, I know, sorry."

Mr. Roark unscrews the top off a bottle of whiskey that's half empty and pours himself a short glass.

"I still think it's a good story though. Here you go, here's some water."

He offers Julia a bottle of water in one hand while holding his glass of whiskey in the other.

Julia doesn't move. She doesn't seem to accept the offering and Mr. Roark looks confused. She just smirks, as if to say, are you kidding me? With her eyes and head slightly cocked sideways. She snatches the glass from his hand and slams the whiskey back with one gulp. Her eyes close as she savors in the moment.

"You might want to grab yourself a glass, and umm, bring the bottle back with you. A year of bottled water, while stuck, trapped in a bunker, and the first day out you don't even offer a girl a drink? Where are your manners, Mr. Roark?"

Julia smiles, signaling to Mr. Roark that she trusts him, and they can both relax now.

"Well okay then."

Mr. Roark grabs the bottle and another glass, and then gently eases back down into the couch. He coughs again and wipes his mouth off slowly, looking to see if there are any new traces of blood.

"I'm sorry, Mr. Roark. I mean, I'm sorry that you are sick. It's pretty bad huh?

"I've lived a good life, Julia. I have no regrets. And I owe Robert for saving my life in Somalia. So, every day I have lived after that, well it has just been a blessing."

He takes a slow, but long drink of whiskey. Julia does the same.

"Why didn't you ever get married, Mr. Roark? And start a family? You would have made a good dad. I mean, you help raise me. And I turned out okay, I think."

"You're better than okay, Julia. Ah, I don't know though. I guess I was just always a loner, you know, and I gave most my life to the military. I thought about it, about getting married, having some kids. It was after we got back, after your dad saved my life. But then I realized I was too much baggage to dump on anyone, and it wouldn't be fair to do that to a family."

Julia closes her eyes and takes another shot of whiskey.

He didn't mean to upset her by his last comment, but he knows it didn't come out right.

"Look Julia, Robert did the best he could as a father and as a husband. We were all messed up from the deployments over the years, you know. I mean we all were. And believe me, I know he wasn't perfect, but you have to know he tried, and that he truly loved you."

"So, does the military teach you guys how to not express your feelings into words? He could have told me he loved us, or me? At least once you know? I don't think that's too much to ask, especially when you know that you may never see each other again. Let's just change the subject okay. You said you would tell me what you know, so start talking."

Mr. Roark nods and refills his glass.

"The bottom line is that there is a group, called The Society, and they have been developing a program to control everyone. Not just in the United States, but every country, worldwide."

"Great. So, I was put in a bunker because of a crazy old man's conspiracy theory, about secret organizations and governments. A nuclear war would have been way easier to believe, to forgive."

Mr. Roark, un-phased by Julia's interruption, continues talking.

"The Society has embedded themselves deep into every major corporation and government over the past century. They are altering and controlling people through a series of flu vaccinations. The first phase was implemented last year, around the same time your dad secured you in the bunker. Your dad didn't know how many it would kill, or what the side effects would be, so he put you in the bunker to keep you as safe and protected as he could. And the rest of us went off the grid until it was safe to resurface, well a little safe anyways."

"But I heard a helicopter when I was leaving the bunker, and nothing seems to be wrong with you, other than your cancer."

Mr. Roark looks up at Julia and raises his eyebrows, questioning her comment.

Julia realizes what she said.

"I'm sorry, that came out wrong. It sounded better in my head."

Mr. Roark slowly reaches over and takes the bottle back from Julia.

"Maybe you should pace yourself? It's been a while since you had a drink."

Mr. Roark pours himself another glass, coughing and almost spilling the whiskey.

"There was a small amount of people that died within seventy-two hours of receiving their flu shot last year. But the majority recovered. They recovered from their normal flu-like symptoms and then continued their daily lives, as normal. But then people began to show signs of different behavior patterns, not drastic but there was still a noticeable change. Then, there are those that didn't receive their shots, and appear to be fine, for now anyways. And last, there are those like me, with a serious illness, that were chosen by The Society to not even be given the chance to receive their virus."

"Wait, what do you mean different behavior patterns? And what about my brother? Is he…?"

"I'm sorry Julia, I don't know. What I do know is that your dad has been networking with other members of our old unit, like me, in hopes that we can find a way to stop this, stop The Society."

Mr. Roark coughs for a few seconds.

Julia sits there quietly. At first, what he was saying sounded completely fictitious to her, but now she couldn't be sure. Mr. Roark appeared to be genuinely honest in what he was saying.

"Sorry. Like I was saying, you know, save-the-world type stuff. So, I figured I'd lend a hand. I didn't really have anything else going on, other than hacking up my lungs and waiting to die, from this cancer."

He stops for a second and smiles at Julia.

"But I think that's enough talk for tonight. How about you take a nice bird bath, and get a good night's sleep? I'm sure you could use it."

Julia sits there for a brief moment, imagining all of the worst possible scenarios about her brother. She gathers her composure, slowly trying to tame the emotional roller coaster she has been on for the past year, especially the past twelve hours. She puts down the glass, nods her head to Mr. Roark, and heads down the hallway, past the slowly burning fireplace.

SIX

Dr. Singer enters his office, with his morning coffee and paper in hand.

"Good morning, Lisa."

"Good morning, Dr. Singer. You have a ten o'clock with Mr. Smith and there are fifteen of your patients scheduled to receive their flu shots today."

"Thank you, Lisa. Hold all my calls please."

Dr. Singer closes and locks his door. He takes a seat and opens the newspaper. He flips to the classifieds section and begins reading. He scrolls down about half way through the page and stops. He circles the two 'For Hire: House Cleaner' posts and copies the numbers down.

- For Hire: House cleaner. Have crew of three cleaners. Awaiting your call. W.A. Shirley. 206-220-1188.

For Hire: House cleaner. Have crew of two cleaners. Awaiting your call. G.A. Allison. 704-312-0879. -

Dr. Singer leans down under his desk and begins to unlock his 'Confidential Patient Files' file cabinet. He removes the files and then pulls a map out. He unrolls the map on his desk and begins to pencil in the numbers '3' inside of Washington, and '2' inside of Georgia. He studies the map and sighs. His head drapes slowly, as if he is disappointed to only find two posts.

There is now a total of twelve states with single digit numbers penciled inside of them on the map. They are somewhat evenly distributed across the map, with just a little less in the east.

Dr. Singer rolls the map back up and seals the filing cabinet. He begins walking to unlock his door but pauses as he passes his window, looking below from six floors high. He begins to stare at the crowds of people that are walking along the busy commerce street. All types of people are walking the city street, just as any other day. But he knows it isn't, just like any other day. It hadn't been like any other day for over a year now. He stares at the scene below him.

People are going to work. People are on their cell phones. People are grabbing coffee at the café. There is a guy running in reflective winter attire with headphones in. There is a woman walking her dog with a litter bag in her hand. And there is a couple kissing beside a cab with the door open. How many of those people are being controlled right now? Dr. Singer asks himself. It made him sick to his stomach when he looked at large crowds of people nowadays.

He breaks from the window and unlocks his office door. He walks back to the window. He looks up at the skyline this time, avoiding the disturbing thoughts about the current situation going on all around him. An office phone begins ringing from outside the room. He looks down at his watch, almost ten o'clock.

"Please hold, Captain Brown." He hears his secretary say.

She knocks on his door and walks in.

"Dr. Singer, Captain Brown is on line one, sir."

"Thank you, Lisa. Tell him I'll call him back in a moment. And close my door please."

"Yes, sir."

Dr. Singer changes out a SIM card on the cell phone from his desk drawer and punches in the phone number.

"Captain?"

"Yes sir, it's me. Line is secure."

"Any up…"

Before he could finish his sentence, Captain Brown interrupts.

"Yes sir, I confirmed the orange panel today. What now? No more stalling Dr. Singer, it's time you tell me what's going on."

Dr. Singer sits quietly with no immediate response. He closes his eyes in relief, now that he knows Julia is safe. He was never overly concerned about her because he knew how strong she was. But he did feel relieved, now that he knew for certain.

"Dr. Singer, hello?"

"I'm here. I'm moving your appointment to this afternoon. We'll discuss everything at three o'clock, Centennial Park.

SEVEN

There is a light buzz of conversations and laughter around the conference room. The large room is filled with government officials, politicians, business executives, doctors and scientists. Several screens display the faces of various Society leaders from around the world. A tall, slightly gray-haired, older gentleman walks in the room and asks everyone if they could please be seated. He sits at the head of the table and then looks at a man to his side, a somewhat younger version of him. The younger gentleman on the left side of the table nods, clears his throat, and begins to speak to the audience.

"Phase three is holding steady at ninety-seven percent effective in all test subjects. All shipments of Phase Two influenza vaccines have been delivered and shots have begun in South East Asia, and in roughly half of the states in America. We still have approximately ninety-eight thousand that have not received Phase One injections yet. Less than ten percent of those are here in the states, and the rest are abroad in various countries. You all have the percentage breakdowns and name lists in your portfolios. Most of the names in the portfolios are affiliated with the nongovernmental anti-vaccination groups. Alternate methods of injections have begun and are projected to be complete within the next six months, and then they will be on track with Phase two or they will be placed on the disposal list."

"Okay Tasha, where are we at with the Phase two messaging?" The gentleman at the head of the table asks.

A breathtaking, beautiful young woman, with perfect auburn hair, raises her head and begins to speak.

"All of the meta-data has been compiled from Phase One. The collection of that data has helped us further track those that have terminal illnesses and who are not to be selected to receive the virus. This targeted selection process will slowly, but effectively, help to eliminate hereditary illnesses within our new civilization. The data has also helped us to 'further identify' those that have not received Phase One shots, by either refusing like those in the anti-vaccination groups, or because they live in remote areas. Refer to your portfolios for by name lists in your respectable areas of location ownership. Phase Two platforms are online, and messages are being sent out already as programmed, social media, blogs, internet ads, television and radio. I'm sure you have all noticed the gradual increase in advertisements and broadcast signal interference. This will continue to increase our ability to track those that are not being controlled. Phase Two implementation will begin to increase specific mission messages on a micro-scale for Phase Three general population testing, and for data collection purposes. And again, just as a reminder, all specific mission messages have to be approved and sanctioned by a majority board member vote. There are plenty of test subjects still available in the population for this, so please, keep sending up requests for your professional, or personal, needs."

All of the members start smiling a little, nodding their heads at one another and taking notes. The woman that just finished speaking looks at the gentlemen at the head of the table and smiles. He acknowledges and gives a wink of approval.

A man from one of the television screens speaks during the brief moment of silence.

"And the Disease Control department, where do we stand there?"

The young woman that was just speaking looks back at the head of the table for approval to speak, but he slightly shakes his head and addresses the man on the television himself.

"Unfortunately, the head of their organization, Mr. Snyder, had a terrible car accident, suffering fatal injuries. So, Mrs. Williams, former head of our Middle East Division, is now in charge of that office. And I assure you, she is fully on board. She has personally guaranteed me that there will be no more issues over there."

Everyone looks around at each other with ease, all seeming to be in acceptance of the response given.

"Okay, everything else is in your binders. Does anyone have anything else to add, for the good of the group? Well, thank you all again for your continued support and hard work."

The audience stands up and place their hands over their hearts for a few seconds, and then lower them. All of the television screens close out and everyone begins to filter out of the room, shaking hands and engaging in light conversations. Everyone leaves except the three that were doing most of the talking during the meeting, the older gentleman, the beautiful woman, and the younger gentleman.

The elder gentleman refills his coffee at the table behind them. The younger gentleman and woman glance at each other, and then the man breaks eye contact.

The man behind them begins to speak, with his back turned towards the two.

"So, where are we at with the non-sanctioned immune bloodlines?"

The young woman gently smacks her lips, just enough to make a sound and then stares at the wall, opposite the young man.

He brushes off her attempt to irritate him.

"Tests are still being done on the infiltrator we caught earlier this year from Disease Control. DNA tests have been traced back to his great-grandfather that was involved in the World War One experiments."

The young man clears his throat, not wanting to continue.

"Based off interrogation of the infiltrator, and after a thorough review of our historical records, there are two more non-Society immune bloodlines than we originally thought. That brings our total to at least five scientists and doctors from the World War One program that are believed to have permanently altered their DNA genes, the genes needed for our virus to work. The infiltrator keeps saying there are more involved that are immune, but five is all we can confirm right now. And just like our current program, the virus they injected themselves with is hereditary and not contagious. It's almost identical to our current immune virus, just a slightly earlier version. Every test we have tried to reverse the infiltrator's immune genes has failed, producing basically the same results from our own immune virus. We inject new DNA strains, but the cells do not survive more than thirty-six hours at most, and then he is back to normal, immune. So, it is slightly different than our immune virus, but the end result is the same, immunity."

He pauses for a moment but the older gentleman motions for him to continue.

"As you know sir, we have been running regular surveillance on forty-nine relatives from the three confirmed bloodlines for years now. But we are still working on tracking down all of the remaining relatives from the two, newly confirmed bloodlines. There were initially fifty-six relatives from the three bloodlines we were already tracking, but seven have since died under various circumstances over the past two years, as you are aware. Three of those being a family in an earthquake in California, two non-related individuals in a terrorist attack in Europe, and two from a plane crash in Tennessee, father and daughter. None of the remaining forty-nine pose a viable threat based off our surveillance. While the relatives from these new, non-Society bloodlines have not been located yet, we don't estimate the number to be high. We only project that number to be anywhere from fifteen to twenty, not a concern for us. And I still recommend that we go with my first recommended course of action, to keep four of them alive for research purposes, two males and two females. And then we can dispose of the remaining non-Society bloodlines gradually over the next year, before we begin Phase Three vaccinations."

The older man looks back the young woman, for her concurrence or disagreement.

"I agree with Michael, Mr. Hardy. But, I would like to be in charge of the disposals. I want to test Phase Two capabilities as much as possible, and this provides an excellent opportunity. I will assign each death mission message to random, individual citizens. This will allow for over forty additional tests to validate Phase Two on the general public. And it will also give us enough time to make any final tweaks to Phase Three, before implementation."

"I'll think about it."

"Sir, I don't think…"

"I said I'll think about it, Mike. Now, I will give both of you my decision tomorrow. That will be all. I have another meeting to get to."

He exits the room, and the two of them stare at each other again.

"Why do you keep insisting on taking unnecessary risks, Tasha? Risking exposing us, when we are so close to controlling everything?"

She walks to the door without responding and then turns, looking back at him just before she exits.

"I have faith in our program, Michael. And I have faith in your father. Don't you?"

EIGHT

Julia is getting frustrated. She keeps trying to dial numbers on the cell phones in the briefcase, trying to contact Brian. 'Not in Service' appears in the signal bar area at the top of the cheaply made, prepaid phone. No touch screen, no internet option, just cheap disposable phones. She slams one of the phones down on the table, frustrated, and begins talking to herself, forgetting that she is not the only that can hear her conversations anymore.

Mr. Roark slowly wakes up, and then begins to move around on the couch as he hears Julia talking to herself. He coughs a couple of times, softly, and then coughs frantically into the blanket. He covers his mouth in an attempt to block the noise, and projectile.

Julia quickly puts the phones back in the briefcase and fixes a glass of water for Mr. Roark, and then walks over to the couch. She gently rubs his shoulder.

"Mr. Roark. Here, here's some water for you."

Mr. Roark attempts rolling over to face her but continues his episode of coughing. After a couple of failed attempts, and finally with some assistance from Julia, he sits up and begins drinking the water.

Julia's face widens.

"Mr. Roark! Let me get you a towel."

Mr. Roark wipes his mouth and sees the dried blood on his hand, mixed with the fresh water. And then he sees the murder scene on the blanket in his lap.

"Come on Tommy, get it together." He says to himself, quietly.

"I'm sorry, Julia. I honestly don't know how much help I am going to be, I can barely fend for myself here. I'm going to bleed out before I help get you out of here."

Julia returns with a towel and another blanket.

"It's okay, Mr. Roark. Taking care of people is something I have experience in. I took care of my mom for ten years, while she prayed to the porcelain gods every night, while my dad was away somewhere. And then she ran off with Trent and ended up dying on his watch. A lot of help he did for her. Sorry, I didn't mean to say that out loud. Here, let me get that blanket."

Julia takes his blanket and sets it to the side. She begins carefully wiping off his face and hands, ringing the blood out of the towel, and then wiping again.

Mr. Roark smiles softly and feels at ease, his coughing suppressed for the moment.

"Those phones aren't set up for outgoing calls. They are only going to work for incoming calls. You know how he is, obviously."

He sees her mind start to race and before she can ask, he changes the subject.

"Anyways, what time is it?"

"About ten," Julia answers back quickly.

"Ten? Did you put the…?"

"Yes, I put the orange panel on the roof this morning when I woke up. Not sure why, but I did. I did what he asked in the letter. I assumed he told you to do it too, just in case I didn't. Right? But I'm pretty sure I should be the one that doesn't trust him, and not the other way around."

Mr. Roark takes another drink of water and changes the subject.

"What time did you wake up?"

"Like, around six o'clock."

"I must have been out cold, must have been more exhausted than I realized. Don't you want to rest? Aren't you tired?"

Julia lowers her head and stares questionably at Mr. Roark, as if to remind him where she has been for the past year.

Mr. Roark apologizes with his eyes.

"Well, did you eat yet?"

"Ate, exercised, and did some personal hygiene. Kind of hard to break a habit in one day. Especially after doing the same routine every day for a year, in order to maintain some kind of, well, some kind of sanity. It felt so amazing to run outside this morning Mr. Roark. And if it wasn't for fear of having a guilty conscious, I would have kept running. But after being left alone for a year, I don't think I could ever do that to someone else, least of all you."

"Well, thank you for coming back my dear. I wouldn't want your dad to kill me before this cancer did."

They both smile. Julia hops up and starts walking back to the kitchen.

"Oh yeah, funny thing, I heard another helicopter flying around this morning while I was running. I heard one yesterday too."

"What time was that?"

"Not long ago, maybe an hour. Why? Wait, is that how we're getting out of here?" Julia asks eagerly. "That's what the panel is for, right? The panel on the roof, it's for the helicopter to come and pick us up, right?

"Well...not exactly. You are going to leave here at some point, but you are going to drive out of here. I've got a vehicle, stashed just a few miles away. The panel is simply a confirmation signal to your dad, so he knows for sure that you are alive and safe. There's no way he would expose this place by landing a helicopter here. He should call any day now though, now that he knows you made it out and are here with me."

Julia's face goes blank, as she stares into nothing and begins to think about her father.

NINE

Captain Brown spots Dr. Singer in the park, sitting on a bench with a newspaper folded out in his lap. He takes a deep breath and stares at him, and his so-normal of an appearance.

Evenly and closely shaven beard, modest business suit, overcoat, glasses, and a well-groomed head of dark hair. Everything looked very clean and professional, very normal looking. Everything about it frustrated Captain Brown. He was so irritated with this man. He couldn't understand how someone this deceiving could look so normal. Yet, there was something comforting to Captain Brown about Dr. Singer, something about just being in his physical presence. Yet another mystery to Captain Brown.

He gathers his thoughts and all of the looming questions race back to his mind, and he makes a straight, fast-paced march toward the bench.

Dr. Singer continues reading and neglects to look up at Captain Brown, now standing almost on top of him. He grabs a briefcase with his right hand and moves it from the bench to beside his feet, still holding the newspaper with his left hand, appearing to still be reading.

"Have a seat, Justin."

"Thanks. Didn't realize we were on a regular first name basis now. Makes me think you might be somewhat normal after all. Bill, is it?"

Dr. Singer casually flips the page of the paper and continues to read.

"Come on, that was a joke man. Never mind. Look, you said were going to tell me everything. If you're not then, well, that's it. You can just…"

Dr. Singer interrupts him.

"My briefcase, pick it up. One. Three. Nine. Twenty-seven. What I am about to tell you, and what you are about to see, is going to be hard to believe at first."

Captain Brown hesitates for a second, and then turns the combination dials. Click. He opens the briefcase and glances up at Dr. Singer. He looks back at the briefcase and begins flipping through the pictures that were on top of several folders and papers, carefully looking at each picture.

The first few were pretty old, and somewhat faded, but still clear enough to recognize what they were. The pictures were of mangled and dismembered men. And they appeared to be wearing old military uniforms. Soldiers, he thought to himself. On the back of one of the photos was a handwritten note, barely legible.

- 1918. Test Subjects 1-3. Time of Injection 0735, 21SEP. Time of Death 2315, 21SEP. -

"The pictures you are looking at are evidence of a secretly controlled zombie program, that is known as T-S-O-M-B-I-E. It's pronounced just like the 'Z' word. The initials stand for, Test Subjects of Mental Behavior Injection Experiments."

Captain Brown's eyes scan back and forth over the photos, his eyes growing wide, and then smaller again. Confusion and disbelief clearly painted on his face. Somewhat speechless, he puts down the photos and picks up a brown leather, pocket-sized notebook. 'R.R.' was engraved on the bottom right corner, barely visible. He begins thumbing through the pages and sees dates at the top of each page. He notices the dates appear to be in chronological order. He realizes that it's a diary.

"That belonged to my great-grandfather. He was in World War One, not as a Soldier though. He was a doctor. He was part of a group that was involved in conducting tests on Soldiers during the war, when the TSOMBIE program first stood up."

"Okay. Well, you certainly have my attention, Dr. Singer."

Captain Brown closes the briefcase, leans back and turns his head, now completely facing Dr. Singer.

"I'm all ears Doc."

Dr. Singer looks at him for a second, then lights a cigarette. He exhales slowly, and then begins talking.

"After the Civil War, there was something of a secret society that was formed, simply known as, The Society. It was founded by a group of wealthy men and women, who essentially wanted to preserve America from killing herself, in the future. The original founder was a young, American entrepreneur. He was traveling on a business venture and came across a voodoo doctor at a local Haitian market. This doctor was able to temporarily control people by using a liquid concoction made from blowfish. The entrepreneur began researching on how to market this potion. But then a war started. He abandoned his business exploration and came back to America after he heard about the Civil War, only to find his family had already been killed. So, he quit his business and got into politics. Shortly after realizing he was good at it, he started a campaign for President. Then him and a couple of his colleagues, who had also lost everything in the war, decided to start an organization. Using what he had discovered in Haiti, this organization would reinvent this serum that could be used to control someone, doing whatever it took to manipulate certain people, and events. They were doing it in order to keep families safe in America, to prevent another Civil War."

Captain Brown is unsure about what he is hearing but doesn't want him to stop talking.

"Over the next decade, The Society slowly began infiltrating, everywhere. First was the government, then private business corporations, and then they infiltrated other secret societies that had more power and reach at the time. They took over the Illuminati, Freemasons, New World Order, and the others. They took over all of the key positions within these organizations first, but they never openly claimed ownership. They recruited scholars, scientists, and of course wealthy elitists, who provided the necessary skills and financial backing of their research and further enhancements of the control serum. The current voodoo-like potion they had at the time was effective, but The Society wanted a more permanent zombie formula. They wanted to manipulate people for longer periods of time. So, they created what was known as the Chemistry Bureau, to develop a virus form of it. This would later evolve into the Food and Drug Administration, ultimately controlled by The Society, with the sole purpose to make the zombie effect permanent. Then, just like they had feared, another war began."

Dr. Singer takes a drink of coffee and lights another cigarette. Captain Brown is deep in concentration, and he blocks out the other noises and everyone else in the park that is walking around.

"World War One provided the perfect platform for The Society to test their enhanced zombie formula, to test it on a larger scale. And the war gave serious justification to The Society's purpose, and ultimately helped them recruit those that were weary of joining their movement before. The war offered up several subjects to conduct experimental tests on. Almost all of the subjects were Soldiers who were severely injured and dying, or were likely to die. So, there was really no objection when they were told they may live longer if they just consent to the tests. Most tests failed immediately. But there were some of their enhanced formulas that seemed to work. The subjects in those cases lived up to a few days after they were given the injection. They were able to fully function and comprehend information, but their speech was impaired, and their motor skills were significantly slower. They looked terrifying. They moved around slowly, but they moved around like nothing was wrong. But something was wrong. They all had these horrid, severely grotesque injuries, and they were just walking around."

Dr. Singer takes a brief pause to light another cigarette. Captain Brown still sits quietly, waiting patiently to hear more.

"Now that America could fall victim to destruction from not only herself, but from other nations, The Society was going to use the TSOMBIE program to create the perfect military. This would be a military in which the Soldiers would be able to continue fighting, long after they were injured. Around this same time, the Spanish flu pandemic hit, as a result of a horrible cross contamination accident with their zombie formula, and it spread rapidly. It was a drastic mistake. The formula was not desired to be viral, because viral meant it would put everyone at risk of being controlled, which included The Society members. After this temporary setback, the group of scientists and doctors that were developing the formula were forced to develop an anti-virus vaccine, a vaccine that would permanently prevent the virus from ever infecting members of The Society. And they did. They developed a permanent anti-virus that increased the cell membrane strength in their bodies, essentially adding an extra layer of protection around their cell membranes, including their brain cells. This actually ended up making them immune to almost any type of cell manipulating virus. This anti-virus prevented the prefrontal cortex cells from being manipulated, or from being controlled."

Dr. Singer pauses for a moment as a group of people closely passes by them.

"After World War One was over, there were rumors circulating about the TSOMBIE program, and the experiments that went on. So, in response, The Society started to manipulate the news media, television and radio, and then the film industry. The Society then began releasing the first ever, zombie movies. They made these movies in order to create a fictional notion about zombies and turn them into unbelievable fairytales that the world would just see as entertainment. And they were right. Shortly after these movies started coming out, the rumors went away. This was just one of their many cover ups of the TSOMBIE program that's been used over the past century though. Around this same time, in the 1930s, the flu vaccination programs began worldwide. The Society saw this as their perfect opportunity to rapidly spread the TSOMBIE virus. Once it was perfected, and they had infiltrated deep enough in every powerful company and government organization, they would release the virus in the form of a flu shot."

Dr. Singer lights another cigarette and takes another drink of coffee, waiting for a family to pass by them.

"The Society wanted to achieve success, but they knew in order to remain a complete secret, they would have to be patient in their efforts. So, we come to World War Two, yet another platform for The Society to conduct zombie trials. But there was something more motivating about them succeeding this time, nuclear bombs. The chance of a nuclear war really forced The Society to go to extreme measures when infiltrating other countries, other groups, or other government branches. And once again, it brought further justification for their existence to current members. And once again, it helped recruit the doubters. This war really made them double their advancements and research efforts with TSOMBIE. After World War Two and the possibility of nuclear war was a permanent reality, The Society realized that they had to do better than create a perfect military. They would create the perfect nation. And that nation would rule the world. America would control all, without anyone ever being the wiser."

Dr. Singer takes a drink of coffee and pauses for Captain Brown to actually say something, to offer one of his sarcastic remarks, but there is just silence. He thinks about stopping but he could tell he seems to believe him, so he continues.

"The Society then infiltrated the Center for Disease Control. It had recently formed, and therefore, it was easy to manipulate, easy to control.

Then they relabeled the Chemistry Bureau to the Food and Drug Administration, in order to move away from the previous World War One rumors and stigma around their zombie experiments. The Worldwide Health Organization caught wind of some suspicious activity, and off-the-record testing that was going on at these factories. So, they created the Global Influenza Surveillance Network in the 1950s. The real intent of this team was to uncover and expose The Society. But after nearly half a century of building up The Society, their reach was just too deep. The Society actually ended up infiltrating the influenza surveillance organization, just shortly after that organization had tried to expose them."

"Over the second half of the twentieth century, The Society began using the flu vaccinations as an embedded cover up. It created the perfect stage in which to mass inject the world, willingly, with their virus. The Society really believed that they would be helping all of mankind and eliminate the chance of a World War Three, if they could succeed with permanent zombification. After continued research and trials, they realized that in order to make the effects permanent by using the flu vaccine, a series, or phase of shots would be needed. This allowed for adequate incubation periods of the virus and cell manipulation. The necessary amount needed to make the effect permanent was just too strong to be given at one time, and ultimately killed the host by over manipulating cells too quick. A phased injection plan of three shots was the solution to permanent cell membrane degradation and manipulation, without killing the host or making them overly zombified."

"Phase One was enough brain cell manipulation to control small patterns of behavior, like eating habits, color choices, and brand selection of products for example. It was enough for The Society to manipulate people without easily being noticed right away. Because the last thing they wanted was for people to catch on that their behavior was changing. People basically carry out their normal, natural thoughts and choices, but on a more frequent and routine basis. People are more susceptible to current trends going on as well. Even if they aren't sure why they like something, if a lot of people like it then they do too, regardless of any previous bias."

"Phase Two injections, going on now, is a strong enough increase to manipulate the prefrontal cortex cells, in order to accept encoded messages from things like media sources, radio, television. This phase incorporates the effects of Phase Three but only temporarily, with the main effect being the loss of freethinking, freewill. During this phase, now that technology has advanced so much, there will be a significant increase in internet marketing, and social media ads and messages. People will be subject to commit certain acts that their subconscious encodes from these messages sent out by The Society."

"And then the final injection to make the zombie effect permanent, Phase Three. These injections were scheduled to be administered a year apart, in line with the annual flu vaccination timeframes. This means we have one year left before Phase Three begins. The last shot will be enough to permanently cement the effects of Phase Two, which means people will have permanent loss of control over their freewill. Their conscious will be dead, but they will be very much alive, and controlled. There will be loss of one's control over their psychological and nervous systems. This will also be controlled by programmed messages sent by The Society. It has taken the Society decades to perfect Phase Three and to make the effects permanent, without killing the host. Around the turn of the century they were gaining traction and had a solution in which the effects lasted a couple of years. The current record is roughly ten years now and holding, and that was permanent enough for the Society to move forward with starting injections on the population. Last year The Society began Phase One injections worldwide, and now we are in the middle of flu season again. Phase Two injections have already been administered in several states and countries already. Within another twelve months we will be living in a world...a world not our own anymore."

Dr. Singer, done with explaining key information to Captain Brown for the moment, takes a long drink of coffee and pulls a new pack of cigarettes from his overcoat, smacking them against his knee a couple of times.

Justin sits in a calm storm of utter shock, confusion, and fear. And while he is fighting to disregard it all, as just conspiracy nonsense, he can't.

Something deep down is telling him that Dr. Singer is telling the truth.

"It's a lot to take in Justin. Take your time. Want a smoke?"

Dr. Singer lights a fresh cigarette and watches the exhale of his breath and smoke, as it mixes with the cold winter air in the open park.

He is taken back by Dr. Singer's calm nature, as if he had known about this TSOMBIE program forever, and it was just a normal part of his life or something. He begins thinking of his wife, Claire, and begins to feel his emotions rising, mixed with anger. Calm down Justin, he tells himself, just relax. I'm in the military for crying out loud, I would have been told something about this. Wouldn't I? He regains composure and control of his internal mind game, and then begins to focus on rationales to discredit this outrageous story he's just been told. He wants to appear calm and not let Dr. Singer see that he is upset.

"No thanks, Bill."

He moves in on the offensive.

"I received my flu shots last year when I was deployed. So, if I am to believe everything you have just told me…then that means I am a zombie too. So why are you asking me for help? And why did you tell me all of this? Aren't you worried that the 'Big Bad Society' will extract the information from me?"

"You don't have the virus, Justin. I ran your blood tests myself. Believe me kid, I wouldn't have anything to do with you if…"

AMERICAN Z

Dr. Singer stops in mid-sentence and shakes his head. He decides not to talk about any more details right then, not in the park. It would soon be dark, and he wants to change the setting to help calm Justin down a little bit.

"And my name is not Bill."

He takes another drag from the cigarette and tosses it in his coffee, and then into the trashcan beside them. He secures his briefcase, stands up, and looks back at the young captain sitting on the bench, by himself.

"Come on. Let's go get a drink, Justin. I still have a lot more that I need to tell you."

Justin, wanting so desperately just to walk away from this man forever, and forget he exists, stands up and begins to walk beside Dr. Singer. Even though he despises him, he believes what he had told him. He thinks about the picture and files in the briefcase and wonders why anyone would go to that much trouble to make up a story. And the whole time he had known Dr. Singer, he had never come off like one to make up stories. So, he goes with him.

The two men walk towards a restaurant and bar district, across the park, in silence.

TEN

"Alright Mr. Roark, here is another stack. I think we have enough wood for tonight, don't you?"

Julia comes in the living room and drops the wood beside the fireplace, scaring Mr. Roark unintentionally out of the chair.

"Sorry, didn't mean to scare you."

Mr. Roark coughs a few times and reaches for his water.

"No, it's okay. I'm fine. Yeah, that's definitely enough. I'll take care of the fire and start making us some dinner. Why don't you go get cleaned up and relax for a bit?"

Julia starts walking out of the living room area when a strange, but once familiar noise starts coming from the briefcase, it is the sound of a cell phone. The two look at each other, and Mr. Roark motions for Julia to answer it. Julia walks over to the kitchen table and stares into the briefcase at the ringing phone, lighting up the dimly lit kitchen. She stares, contemplating on whether or not to answer it. She knows who is on the other end. What am I going to say?

She had thought about this moment over and over again in her head for the past year. But in her mind this conversation would always happen in person, not over the phone. In her mind it would always end with her smacking him, and then him hugging her and telling her how sorry he was, and then they would both cry.

Wake up Julia, snap out it, she says to herself. This is your dad we are talking about here, not a caring father.

She picks up the phone, hits the talk button, and presses it firmly to her ear, not saying anything.

"Tommy, is that you?"

When there is no immediate response he realizes that Julia is the one that has answered.

He has thought about what he would say to her when they talked again, and how he would try to apologize without seeming like a jerk.

Now is that time. And he knows he has delayed this call long enough.

"Julia, I can't begin to say how sorry I am. I know you probably hate me right now, for doing what I did. But in my defense, I did what had to be done, to ensure you were safe. We can't talk long on these phones, but after Mr. Roark thinks you are ready we will see each other. And I promise I will explain everything to you then, in person."

Julia is controlling her emotions better than she thought she would. Maybe it is because it is happening over the phone and not face to face, she thinks.

She clears her throat and thinks about saying something, but instead she hands the phone over to Mr. Roark and walks away.

Mr. Roark takes the phone, feeling sorry for Julia and what she must be going through right now.

He walks with the phone to the back door and steps outside on the porch.

"Hey, I'm here."

Julia stares out the window at Mr. Roark carrying on a conversation with her dad. She wakens herself from a temporary paralysis and grabs the bottle of whiskey off the table. She takes the bottle to the bedroom and closes the door.

Mr. Roark comes back in and puts the phone in the briefcase. He sees the bottle of whiskey missing from the table. He walks back to the bedroom and knocks on the door.

"Julia, I know you're upset. I...I'm here to help Julia. But if you won't talk to me, can you at least share the alcohol?"

Mr. Roark coughs a few times, and then he throws in a few more unnecessary coughs, in an effort to attract pity.

Julia opens the door, takes the glass from his hand, and fills it to the top. She tilts her head sideways as if asking, are you happy now? Then she closes the door abruptly in his face, and his smile turns into a smirk.

"Okay. Thanks. I guess I'll let you know when dinner is ready then."

Mr. Roark walks back to the living room and utters under his breath while taking a drink, "And that's why I am glad that I don't have kids."

ELEVEN

"A shot of tequila please."

Dr. Singer quickly slams a shot at the bar after coming out of the restroom. He then returns to the booth with Captain Brown. He takes a seat and gulps the glass of whiskey that is there waiting for him.

Justin takes a small sip of his drink and raises his hand to the waitress for another round, as if to beat Dr. Singer to the punch.

Dr. Singer pulls out his cigarettes and lights one. He reaches across Justin and pulls out the ashtray from the back of the table. He takes a good look around the half empty restaurant. He doesn't notice anyone that is not infected, and everything appears to be ordinary, as ordinary as it could be. He smokes the cigarette and feels that it's safe for them to stay there for a while.

"Everything alright?"

Justin asks with a chipper voice, almost enthusiastic. It actually makes him happy to see this man who was always so cool and calm, now appear to be rattled, upset and emotional.

Dr. Singer picks up on Justin's tone and quickly regains his composure and the task at hand, finishing the details of The Society and the

TSOMBIE program. He takes a toke from the cigarette and exhales.

"Here you gentlemen go. Can I get you anything to eat?" The young waitress asks, as she sits another glass down and makes eye contact with Captain Brown.

"Are you in the military?"

"Yes ma'am. I'm a pilot, helicopter pilot."

"It's nice to see grown men who still go out with their parents."

She looks over at Dr. Singer.

Justin almost spits his drink out.

"Uh, ha, yeah, we are not related." Justin fires back quickly. He looks up at the ceiling with his eyes closed and utters under his breath, "Thank. You." He lowers his head back down and takes a drink a whiskey.

"We're fine. Just keep the drinks coming, thank you." Dr. Singer mumbles out rudely, with his head looking into the, now empty, glass of whiskey.

Captain Brown smiles apologetically at the waitress, as she turns and walks away.

Dr. Singer realizes he is still being emotional. He decides to calm himself and begin a casual conversation, to ease back into the point of the meeting.

"So, Mr. Pilot, how do you like flying? We never really talked about it during your physical therapy."

Justin pauses for a moment at the unfamiliar conversation tone.

"I like it, I guess. It's a career, an honest and respectable job. It's not as fun as it was when I first started flying, now it feels more like a nine-to-five sometimes. But I still enjoy it."

Dr. Singer doesn't appear he has anything else to add, so Justin decides to continue talking, feeling a little bit at ease now with the topic of conversation.

"Ever since I could remember, I wanted to be a pilot. I lived near a farm growing up, and when I got old enough our neighbor would let me ride with him, in his crop duster. After that first ride I was hooked."

Justin pauses for a moment, thinking about the memories he had as a kid, and then takes a drink.

"What about you, Dr. Singer? Do you like your career? Do you like being a doctor?"

"I'm not a doctor, Justin." He takes a drink and pauses for a moment. "I used to be a pilot though."

Justin sits his glass on the table, looking somewhat confused.

"I used to be a lot of things. Soldier, pilot, husband." He looks at the glass. "Father."

Dr. Singer raises his glass to Justin, "Here's to flying though, huh?" He finishes the last sip in his glass and then lights another cigarette.

"You're not a doctor? I don't get it. How did I get referred to you by the military for physical therapy then? I've been to your office. I've seen your degrees. Hell, I've even searched you on the internet. It all checked out to me."

"It's a cover, Justin, just a cover. I used to fly for the military in my real life, special operations. A little different than the type of flying you do, but still much the same."

"But the internet says you started your practice in the 90's. And your degrees, they were all dated before then. So how did you...?"

"It was a lot easier to forge documents back then, Justin. We didn't have this all-knowing internet that your generation has become clung to, like some kind of alternate life source. I started the cover life of Dr. Singer after I returned from Somalia in the early 90's. I still continued my day job as a military pilot though. But being in special operations back then, well our missions were few and far between. We had a lot more 'off duty' time, and that allowed me to run the cover life simultaneously."

He sees this as the opportunity to continue with the original point of being there, to tell Justin more details about The Society and TSOMBIE program.

"When I was in Somalia, I came across a lot of secret squirrel types, non-military mostly. Most were just assumed to be the three letter agency types that we normally dealt with. But then this one group took all of our evidence and detainees we secured after an operation, no questions asked. And it was cleared by everyone from command. This one gentleman from that group approached me and said he remembered me from a few years ago in South America. And then he told me that he knew how my father really died. He said he would be in touch with me when I got home, back stateside. Half of me believed him and the other half, well, back then I honestly just didn't care. He was never much of a father to me when he was alive, you know, sob story crap."

"So, a few months after I had returned home and got back into the normal groove of things, the gentleman from Somalia, Dr. Nichols, shows up at my house. He tells me this unbelievable story about this organization he works for, the one my father also worked for, and then was killed when he tried to leave. He told me things about my father, and about me, that nobody else could have known. So, there was no reason to doubt he knew my father, but I didn't buy his story about this Society that he was part of. He also told me that they had a record on my entire family. They had records on everyone's family that had ties with The Society. He told me The Society had infiltrated every intelligence organization. And then to convince me even more, he showed me pictures of me and my wife, on our vacation. Then he pulls out this little brown diary, and I was speechless. I was angry, and I was sad, all at once. I didn't know how to take it at first. I wasn't sure why he was telling me all of this anyways, because he obviously stood the risk of getting us both killed, if this Society was really what he claimed them to be."

Dr. Singer looks at the door of the bar opening up and watches the new patrons come in. He watches them go to a table and open their menus.

Infected.   No threat.   He lights a cigarette and continues talking.

"The diary, as I mentioned a minute ago, it belonged to my great grandfather, the same one from the World War One experiments. He was not just a doctor, he was actually a member of The Society, and he brought his son and grandson, my father, into it as well. The Society recruits heavily from within their own family, to increase trust, and reduce being compromised or betrayed by one of their own. Then he showed me the letter that my father wrote before they killed him. The letter was addressed to me. My father's letter explained how he didn't want my life to be ruined because of The Society, like his was. Their beliefs had become too immoral for him to continue to be a loyal member. He wanted me to be proud of him. He didn't want me to be ashamed of him, for what this group would do to the world. Dr. Nichols had me. I was all in after that. I volunteered to help him and his efforts to stop The Society. I admit, I wanted a little revenge, but in the same token I wanted to continue what my father started, to do something that would make him proud as well."

"Dr. Nichols was mentored by my father in The Society, and he too had been brought in through his family. He agreed with my father, that The Society had become too egregious in their ambitions, and that they were going too far with the TSOMBIE program. Dr. Nichols and I were roughly the same age. He despised his father for this way of life he was brought into, so our issues we had with our families connected us.   And we understood each other's motivations. I had a little knowledge about subversion with my special operations background, but I wasn't a door kicker. And I wasn't an expert on the interpersonal-level, tradecrafts of covert operations. So, he began teaching me the art of infiltration. And then I began my cover life as Dr. Singer."

Dr. Singer knows Justin wants to ask what his real name is. And he waits, but Justin doesn't ask.

Justin realizes that Dr. Singer would eventually tell him his real name, as he is telling him everything now. So, he stays quiet and listens as Dr. Singer continues.

"We knew that any chance we had at stopping or slowing down The Society was to fully understand the vaccine, to track the progress, and to understand the effects it had on people. The best way to do that was in the medical field. That way, we would have direct access and knowledge on the flu shots being administered. I bounced back and forth between my two lives over the years. I started a family and retired from the military in one, and I continued as a recluse, single doctor in the other. We also took the necessary precautions over the years to protect our families. We built underground bunkers in the event that Phase One failed and killed people by the masses, or worse, created a plaque with unintended side effects. Dr. Nichols continued to move up in the ranks in The Society research facilities, getting closer and closer to gaining a position at the main laboratory. Finally, after years of strategic planning and preparation, he was in. He was nominated as the director of the main research laboratory at American Global Incorporated, or AGI, the main business cover corporation of The Society."

"We tried to sabotage The Society's efforts and advancements a couple of times over the years. Each time we failed though, only to learn that there were contingent supplies of the vaccine and only the key leaders of The Society knew where they stored. The production and research would slow down for a few days after one of our failed attempts. Then they would just ship in the new supplies and just like that, they were back up and running again. Unfortunately, there were some innocent lives that had to be sacrificed in order for us to continue our efforts. If they ever suspected Dr. Nichols of anything, then well, our game was up. We have done things we are not proud of Justin, but we did what had to be done. We had to do something and at least try to save our country, our world."

A loud shattering of glass from the kitchen behind the bar breaks the conversation. Dr. Singer and Justin both look at where the noise came from and then see a waiter rolling a mop bucket to the kitchen. Seeing everything is okay, Dr. Singer continues talking.

"Then last year, Phase One began and we proceeded with our original plan of sheltering our families in the bunkers. The best way to keep The Society or anyone from hunting you, is to make them believe you are dead. So, I faked my daughter's death, along with my death, in a private plane crash. My wife, ex-wife, had already died before this started. My son was also out of the picture already, living with his step-father. I was unable to keep my marriage together over the years, as was Dr. Nichols. So, I put the only piece of me I had left in a bunker, my daughter. And then I simply went back to work the next day, as Dr. Singer, as if nothing had ever happened."

"Dr. Nichols' son was the only thing he still cared for in this world, just like how I felt about my daughter. His son was too young to go into a bunker by himself though. So, the plan was to keep him from getting the shot. But he was too late, and he was unable to keep his son from getting injected with Phase One. His ex-wife had travelled out of state and got the shots before he could tell her not to. He was traumatized. I got him back on track before The Society got suspicious of his absence or of his depressed behavior at work. And then we went back to work on trying to stop the other phases from happening, for his son, for everybody."

"Miss, can we get another round?" Justin raises his voice a little more to the inattentive waitress. "Hello, Miss, can we get another round?" Justin now reaches out to the waitress cleaning the table beside them, who appears to be completely tuned out to his voice.

She snaps around quickly when he touches her.

"Sorry. I didn't mean to scare you there. Can we get another round? And I think we would like something to eat too, could you bring us a couple of burgers please?"

"Sorry, I must have zoned out there for a second. Two burgers, sure. Are you sure you want burgers? Everyone normally orders the wings here."

"Burgers are fine, thank you."

She walks away with a blank expression on her face.

Dr. Singer lights another cigarette. "Another victim." He takes a long, slow drag, and then waves the pack of cigarettes at Justin before he puts them down on the table.

Justin looks at him and then he stares at the pack of cigarettes on the table.

"Alright, let me have one. I'm down to just one smoke at the end of every day. But I'm on borrowed time anyway, right? So, I guess it really doesn't matter how much I smoke anymore, does it?"

He lights a cigarette and sits back in the booth, waiting for Dr. Singer to continue.

Dr. Singer takes another drink and clears his throat.

"So, months go by and Dr. Nichols continues making the effort to visit his son, feeling guilty for ever letting this happen to him. Then he begins to notice something. His son isn't showing signs of Phase One behavior patterns. At first, he thinks maybe it's just his optimism, his mind playing tricks on him. But then he begins conducting blood tests on his son, the same ones he did in the lab on the TSOMBIE subjects. It was unbelievable when he looked at the results. His son's blood did not test positive for Phase One. Thinking that maybe it was a flawed shipment or something along those lines, he runs the same tests on his ex-wife. But she is no doubt, infected with Phase One. He tracks down the hospital where they received the shots from and verifies the vaccine numbers, and verifies other patients, and they were all infected. His son did not have Phase One, but he received the same vaccine as everyone else did. So why wasn't he infected?"

Justin leans forward, more intrigued.

"Up to this point, over our years of research, we knew a few things that were certain about the virus. We knew that the virus was not contagious, meaning it could not be spread airborne or by bodily fluids. We knew that people with certain diseases were not selected to receive the virus in the first place. This was mainly because it sped up the death in people that were already terminal by weakening their cell membranes. And we also knew that there were two types of the anti-TSOMBIE vaccine, temporary and permanent. The temporary anti-virus was used on new Society member candidates, the ones that showed potential of becoming official members. The Society held the permanent shot over their head as an incentive to do whatever was asked of them. The permanent anti-virus was, and still is, guarded very close. Only the top leadership of The Society has access to it. The permanent anti-virus is only given to members after they are voted in and are deemed essential Society members. And now, because of Dr. Nichols testing his son's blood, we understand why The Society has always been so strict about who received the permanent anti-virus. The TSOMBIE permanent anti-virus is hereditary."

"Excuse me gentlemen."

The waitress sits the two plates down on the table.

"Can I get you anything else?"

Justin is speechless from Dr. Singer's conversation at this point and says nothing.

"Just the check," says Dr. Singer.

The waitress gives another blank stare to them and then walks away.

"Hereditary?"

Dr. Singer can see Justin's mind working hard, trying to process the information dump he just laid on him. He begins eating his burger and decides to let him work through it at his own pace.

"Before, you said that all of the doctors involved in the World War One experiments had injected themselves with an anti-virus, to keep them safe from getting contaminated with the virus. So, was their version of the anti-virus back then hereditary as well? Or did Dr. Nichols receive the permanent anti-virus from being a member of The Society? And if the original anti-virus was hereditary…then that means you can't get infected either, right? Your great grandfather was involved in the first experiments, so he would have received the anti-virus too, right?"

"Dr. Nichols was told he was given the anti-virus, but The Society tells that to all their members, so there's no way to know for sure if he was actually given the real permanent version."

Dr. Singer takes a long pause. He wants to avoid answering Justin's other question for the moment, regarding his family and immunity bloodlines. He decides to shift the focus back to Justin.

"So, I ran tests on your blood last month, and like I said before, you're clean, Justin."

Justin sits quietly for a moment, thinking hard.

"So, someone in my family was in The Society? Or they still are in The Society? But how would that help...knowing my family was in The Society? I don't see how this could prove your theory of it being hereditary, and not just a bad batch of shots or something. Maybe those Phase One shots didn't make it to my unit overseas, on my deployment. Did you ever think of that? I mean I got it, The Society is almighty and powerful. But that is still a lot of coordination for every batch of flu shots to arrive on time and work, every single time. My point is, there still has to be a margin of error. I may not be a doctor or scientist, but I at least know that much."

Dr. Singer sees that Justin has gone from interested to agitated. He decides that this is enough for one night, and he wants to give him some time to decompress and really digest everything.

"You're right, Justin. A margin of error cannot be ignored as a possibility. Look, the bottom line is that we are outnumbered in this battle and we need all of the non-infected people we can get on our side. And our time is quickly running out. Think about everything we talked about and let me know your decision in a couple of days. And I will understand if you say no. And I will still try to help you anyway I can, even if you don't join us."

Justin thinks about what he said and takes his last drink. Dr. Singer leaves cash for the bill on the table and they exit, into the somewhat empty city street. Dr. Singer lights a cigarette outside and Justin stands for a moment, in silence. They exchange eye contact for a minute and then they both turn their backs and walk away, without exchanging any goodbyes.

TWELVE

"Good morning Tasha," young Mike Hardy says, with a chipper and excited voice.

Tasha pauses in her step and then starts to walk over to the breakroom kitchen counter where he was standing. She recognizes the happiness in his tone and demeanor as he finishes a drink of coffee, and then refills his cup. Tasha sees that he is gloating in the fact that his father sided with him. His father chose to wait until after Phase Three before he would authorize the elimination process of bloodlines.

"I'm fine, Michael. How are Melissa and the kids?"

Tasha wants to bring him down a bit by bringing up a point of contention, in which she maintains the upper hand.

He puts the coffee pot back and remembers that Tasha still holds his marriage in her hands. He wishes he could do anything to take back that one night. He quickly tones down his demeanor and goes back to a more polite and submissive Mike Hardy.

"They're fine, Tasha. Thank you for asking."

He takes another sip of coffee, trying to appear relaxed after her attempt to rattle him.

Tasha moves in beside him and takes the coffee pot out, while gently brushing against his shoulder. He moves just enough to break contact.

He glances down and pauses at her display of cleavage, right at the top of her business suit.

Tasha was an insanely beautiful woman, there was no denying it. Her physique was mesmerizing, and she could put almost any man into a trance-like state with her beauty alone. After their one night together, he compared her beauty to that of a wild rose, flawless in appearance but concealing many thorns that would quickly sink in your skin should you touch it. It was no secret that she manipulated men with her seductive methods, but that still didn't stop him from going home with her one time. She tried her act with his father, Michael Hardy, Senior, but he was too self-absorbed to ever really care about anyone else. He used her for sex, on and off, but that was it. Everyone had their own purpose and place in his father's eyes.

"Tell Melissa I said hello. We have to get together sometime for dinner, or a shopping date. She's an incredible woman, Michael. She's so cute and talented with her little paintings."

Tasha grins and faces him, holding her mug in one hand and rubbing her necklace, slowly around the top of her low-cut suit with the other.

The day was just getting started and Mike Hardy had received his fill of taunting conversation.

He nods his head to her request, "Will do." Then he turns and exits the break room as if he had somewhere important to be, trying his best not to give her the satisfaction of seeing him in distress.

Tasha gently blows the steam from her coffee and smiles to herself, knowing she still has control over him. "Bye, Michael," she says softly.

* * *

Mike Hardy walks down a flight of stairs and through a series of hallways until he comes to a dead end. He lifts his hand and scans his index finger, awaiting a green light. Then a display of numbers appear on the touch-screen pad. He enters a series of pin code numbers into the pad, and another green light shines. 'Access Granted' displays and then the door unlocks. He enters a long corridor and repeats the process at another door. He enters a stage-like room with a large projector screen that is displaying multiple images, still shot photos, real-time news feeds, drone feeds, and maps.

Hardy takes a look around his large surveillance department room and motions for someone to come to him. He walks though the room to a corner office with glass walls, overlooking the room full of Phase Three analysts plugging away at their computers. He holds the door open for the man he motioned for when he first walked in, his right-hand analyst and personal assistant.

"Good morning, sir."

The young analyst hands him two folders. One with the label, 'Last 24 / Next 24.' And the other has the label of, 'SIGNIFICANT.'

"Thanks," says Hardy, as he takes a seat along the edge of the desk.

"Run me through the significant folder first."

The analyst opens his copy of the folder.

"Yes sir. We picked up more talk of an engagement for, BL-15, Mr. Tumblin. His fiancé is still in graduate school. And although we don't have any real evidence or reason to believe she wants to start a family anytime soon, I still do not think we should take any chances with her."

"Agreed. Send it over to the Network Communications Department. Upgrade her messaging package to Advanced Non-Reproductive Path."

"Yes, sir. There are also some flight itineraries that we are tracking, BL-12, BL-19, BL-35, and BL-42. There are a couple of those that are stateside and two are international, nothing unusual though. They all fall in line with our standard holiday travel estimates. That covers the significant events sir for the bloodlines, sir. As far as the last twenty-four and next twenty-four hours, we are continuing to monitor Phase Two mission success rates of key government personnel. And we are also continuing routine surveillance of all bloodlines in preparation for the upcoming holidays."

"Thanks, Chris. Good update."

Hardy closes the folder and hands it back to the analyst.

"We have a new directive I need to go over with you. Our department is going to increase surveillance operations significantly over the next year, specifically for the bloodlines that are not members of The Society."

He pauses for a moment, giving the analyst time to finish recoding his notes.

"I want metadata compiled for all online and phone activity, and social contact activity. Put teams on all first person direct contacts and family members. Conduct cell phone and email monitoring on all of their second and third-party contacts."

Hardy pauses again, and the analyst looks up at him from his paper.

"Sir, that is…we are going to need another section to be stood up to accomplish this. We are stretched thin due to the increased travel surveillance for the next two months."

"Absolutely. Approved. Put in the request for whatever we need to make this happen. This is a priority for the Inner Circle, Chris."

"Understood. I'll get started right away, sir. Is there anything else, Mr. Hardy?"

"Yes, there is."

Hardy stands up and approaches the young man, placing his hand on his shoulder.

"Nothing, I mean nothing, gets passed to Network Communications without my approval. Every request will personally be vetted, by me, before anything is sent to them. And you will notify me immediately if there are any unauthorized messages, or upgrades, to the non-Society bloodlines. This is critical, Chris."

Hardy smiles and removes his hand from the young man's shoulder.

The analyst finishes writing his notes and then nods, "Understood, sir."

"Good, go brief up the team and get to work. I'll be waiting for the additional section requests."

Hardy walks behind his desk and takes a seat, looking out of the glass windows and into the large department of surveillance analysts, as his assistant exits.

* * *

Tasha McNeil is looking out of an office glass window and into her department, from the chair at the head of her table. Her table is filled by several staff members of her team. There's a man standing at the opposite end of the table with a small screen behind him that has several graphs and charts on it.

"As you can see here, ma'am, there has been a positive trend of ninety-seven percent in social media messaging and tasks accomplished. Television and internet advertising remain just below that, at ninety-six percent. Email and radio have shown a negative trend and are still showing to be the least effective at ninety-four percent. Again, we equate this to inactive email accounts and lack of radio listeners, compared to use of internet and digital media libraries. Over the past..."

Tasha interrupts the man. "Do I have an accent?"

"Um, I'm sorry, ma'am. Do you have an accent?"

"I know you are sorry but that is not what I asked. Do, I, have, an, accent?

The man clears his throat. "No ma'am, no accent."

Tasha stands up slowly, looking at everyone in the room as they try to avoid eye contact with her.

"Well, do I have a speech impediment then?" She asks very calmly, as she looks out of the window into her department's communication center again.

"No, ma'am."

"Do I stutter? Or do I speak regularly in another language other than English?" Again, she speaks calmly, as she now begins walking slowly across the room, looking down at her shoes and then at the table of staff members.

"No, ma'am."

"So, you understand what I say, when I talk?"

"Yes, ma'am."

She stops and locks eye contact with the man.

"Then why do I have to keep repeating myself in these damn meetings!"

The man breaks eye contact and looks at the floor, in shame, in fear.

She looks back at the staff members around the table, all with their heads down, none daring to look up. She begins to walk slowly again, gently dragging her glossy red fingernails over the shoulders of the staff as she passes them. She makes her way to the end of the table.

"I gave very clear instructions at the last meeting," she now says in a calm, soothing voice. "And those instructions were not followed. Now that we know it was not because of my speaking ability, I can only see it as willful disobedience, or, incompetence."

She pauses and looks back at the table, then continues to walk.

"Either way, failure will not be tolerated in my department, in AGI."

She is now standing behind the briefer at the end of the table. She breathes gently into his ear. She closes her eyes in some twisted sense of satisfaction as she feels his body twitching with nervousness against hers. After a brief moment, she opens her eyes and moves in front of the man, between him and the table, facing the staff members.

"Now, does everyone remember what I said at the last meeting? Now that you have all had a chance to reflect."

The staff eagerly move their heads up and down, signaling understanding, and then look at her in silence.

"Great!" She says loud and enthusiastic, sending a wave of body trembles through the staff.

"See you all at the next meeting."

The staff quickly exit their seats and overcrowd the entrance of the door, trying to leave the room. Tasha turns and blocks the briefer from leaving, with her arms crossed.

"Brad, Brad, Brad. What are we going to do about your performance?"

"I promise, I…"

"Ah-ah-ah. Shh." She says, as she gently taps her index finger against his shaking lips.

"You are going to help me with a little project Brad, just me and you. And you must not tell anyone of this. You are going to help with this, or I will make sure that your family lives the rest of their lives as Society factory slaves, at the bottom of the food chain. And you will be given the permanent anti-virus, to ensure you get the full experience of how pitiful life can be. Now, is that clear enough for you to understand?"

"Yes…yes, ma'am." He says, as his bottom lip quivers at full speed.

"Excellent!"

Tasha straightens up his collar and tie and then gently pats his shoulders.

"Now, let's go over some accidental death and kill messaging packages."

THIRTEEN

"Hometown?" Mr. Roark asks.

"California...Los Angeles, California."

"Married?"

"Single."

"Where did you go to college?"

"I did my undergrad in Kansas, graduate in Tennessee."

"Brothers or sisters?"

Julia doesn't reply. She gazes at the table with a daydream-look in her eyes.

"Brothers or sisters?" Mr. Roark asks again.

"Umm, sorry, no…I'm an only child."

Mr. Roark knows that she is thinking of Brian and that she is worried about him.

"Alright. Let's take a little break, huh? I could use a drink and a little shuteye before dinner. We'll start back after dinner with review of common hospital terminology, and how to draw blood. You're doing good Julia, I mean Dr. Gordon. See, even I don't get everything right the first time."

Mr. Roark smiles just a little, at his attempt to get a smile out of her. Unsuccessful, he gets up and starts walking back toward the living room.

"So, how long are we going to be here, Mr. Roark?"

"Well, you're smart, Julia, you always were. I don't think it will take you long to pick up the basics, and then it's just up to your dad after that. When he's ready for you, he will let us know. You're going to get the real crash course from him though. Your dad is a smart man you know."

Mr. Roark sits down softly into the couch and reaches for the glass, with about one half of a shot of alcohol left in it from the night before. He shakes it a bit, finishes what's left in the glass, and then coughs for a brief moment into a fresh hand towel.

Julia had left a stack of towels on the couch, after the incident from the first morning.

Julia grabs a bottle of water and walks over to the couch. She fills his empty glass and places two pills in his hand.

"Take these. I found them in the cabinet. The expiration date is still good on them."

Mr. Roark takes the pills and then coughs for a few more seconds, and then calms himself.

"Okay, I think I'm good now, just going to lay down for bit. Thank you, Julia. I'll be up for dinner though. I don't want to miss your cooking."

"Well, you can get pretty creative when you're stuck with only canned food for a year."

Julia moves back into the kitchen and looks out of the small window, over the sink. She sees a doe and her fawn walking slowly outside. She looks back at Mr. Roark lying down, with the blanket now over his face. She turns back to the deer and watches them graze as they walk along the edge of the tree line. Memories of hunting with her brother start to run through her mind.

- She remembered that day well. It was actually the last day she saw Brian after her mother had died. She relived this memory almost every day during her first few months in the bunker. Trent and his new wife brought Brian to Gatlinburg. That was about half of the distance to drive between them and her father. Brian was turning twelve soon and Trent and his new wife had both agreed that he was old enough to hunt now. Brian was so excited to finally go hunting for the first time. Trent and his wife left right after dropping Brian off, and it was just the three of them in alone in the woods for the weekend. That weekend was the last time she seen Brian. Julia and Brian spent the weekend laughing and talking, about anything and everything. Her dad cooked them breakfast and dinner, but he let Julia do all of the target practice and site selections for hunting. He probably only said about ten words the whole weekend. "Good Morning. Good Night. You hungry? You need anything?" That was about the extent of the family conversation. She remembered that her dad would leave every night and come back early in the mornings. The lights would always wake her up in the morning. She remembered seeing another set of lights too. She remembered seeing Mr. Roark and another one of his military buddies that she recognized, but she couldn't remember his name. Until now she had never given much thought to where he went every night, or what her dad and his buddies were doing. At the time, she figured they were all just drinking at a local bar and she never thought anymore of it. Her focus was on Brian that weekend anyways. But now, after everything that Mr. Roark had told her, she began to think more about what they were actually doing back then. -

She pauses her memory and glances over at Mr. Roark on the couch. Why would he drive almost four hours just to hang out and drink? She asks herself. I'm going to ask him about it when he wakes up. She turns back to the window and begins watching the deer again, starting her memory again.

- They didn't see a single deer that weekend, not until the last afternoon, after they were done hunting and walking back to the cabin. Julia dropped to a knee and took aim on a big doe, but Brian pulled down her rifle barrel. She knew then that he really didn't care about hunting. He just wanted to spend time with her. They both sat in silence as they watched two small deer come up and began playing and frolicking around. The doe stood strong and bold as she watched her two fawns, jumping around and chasing each other. -

Now, Julia stands at the sink, watching this young doe and her one fawn. No playing, no frolicking, just eating in silence. Damn you dad, she says to herself, hitting the counter. The deer both perk up as if they hear Julia smack the countertop, and then with a couple of graceful leaps, they are gone. Julia tries to take some pleasure from seeing the deer. She exhales deeply now that the moment is over and begins preparing dinner.

FOURTEEN

Captain Brown sits quietly in his driveway after driving back home from work.

Since his last meeting with Dr. Singer, Justin had turned into a recluse at work and at home, lost in deep thought within his own mind. He loved Claire, and he loved his Soldiers, his friends. He thought somehow by limiting his conversation and social interaction with them that it would erase the last couple of days or prove Dr. Singer wrong somehow. He just wanted everything to go back to how it was, before he met Dr. Singer. But still, deep down, he believed Dr. Singer and knew his life was going to be different from now on. Justin had spent the past couple of days analyzing every memory of Claire over the past year, dwelling on everything that seemed different or out of the norm. She had definitely changed over the past twelve months, there was no denying that. But he thought it was just her way of getting over the miscarriage.

Eating habits. Almost every meal was repeated on a routine basis. He didn't mind, he thought it helped reduce her stress about cooking different meals all the time. She definitely increased her electronic use over the past year. Now that he was analyzing everything, he could barely remember a time that she didn't have a cell phone or tablet in her hands, constantly texting or reading. He could only see everything Claire did as somehow being weird now, as he stared at her through the living room window from inside his truck.

He watches her go back and forth, from looking at her phone and then to the television, and then back to the phone. He pulls out a cell phone from his dash and inserts a SIM card.

"Hello? It's me Justin...Yeah, I thought it over, and I'm in...Okay...Yeah, I know where it's at...Okay."

Justin hangs up the phone. I pray, I really pray that you're wrong about all this, he says to himself while looking at Claire through the window again. He smokes a cigarette and then walks inside the house.

FIFTEEN

Julia closes the front door softly, trying not to wake Mr. Roark. She walks slowly past him and to the bathroom, for a bird bath after her morning jog. She finishes her morning routine and sits at the kitchen table with a cup of instant coffee, bowl of oatmeal, and can of fruit. I'm so ready to eat real food, she thinks to herself. And drink a real coffee.

She finishes eating her bland breakfast in silence, looking over at Mr. Roark, waiting for him to wake.

He slept through dinner and it was almost nine o'clock, the next morning, and he was still asleep.

She moves to the living room and takes a seat in the chair beside the couch, drinking her coffee and watching the blanket move up and down with his breathing. She intentionally takes a loud exaggerated sip of coffee, and then lets out a long, "Ahh," sigh of refreshment.

It works. His head moves a little, and then he slides the blanket from over his face.

"Good morning," Julia says, with his face still turned from her and in the couch cushion.

He lets out a low mumble and coughs as he starts to rollover and face her. The blanket is covered with blood again. Julia puts down the coffee, no longer smiling, and begins to care for him.

"Your forehead is burning up."

She goes to the bathroom and comes back with a couple of fresh hand towels and a bottle of water. She wets the small towels and cleans his face. She goes to the kitchen and comes back with two more pills in her hand.

"Mr. Roark, Mr. Roark. I need you to sit up for a second."

Julia helps raise him up enough to swallow the pills, and then lowers him back down. She puts a clean wet cloth on his forehead.

"Mr. Roark, you're on fire! You need a doctor, Mr. Roark."

Mr. Roark coughs a couple of times.

"I guess I'm in luck then, Dr. Gordon."

"You know what I mean, a real doctor."

"Sorry, bad joke, I know. What time is it anyway?"

"Nine o'clock."

"Did you eat dinner already?"

"Nine in the morning, Mr. Roark. You slept through dinner, can't you remember? You can't see that it's daylight outside? The hell with staying off the grid, we have to get you to a hospital. Come on."

"No!" He coughs out. "Can't."

"Well, we have to do something. I am not just going to sit here and watch you die, just to what? Just to keep this cabin, you, me, everybody, a secret? I won't do it!"

inside. She packs some food and water. Lastly, she brings another fresh towel and another blanket to Mr. Roark before she leaves.

"I'll be back as fast as I can," she says, looking back at him on the couch before exiting the door.

"Yep, I'll be right here. Be careful."

She closes the door and takes a deep breath as she looks at the forest ahead of her.

She comes upon Mr. Roark's SUV about an hour later, after a mix of walking and light jogging. It is a late 90's model, Sport Utility Vehicle, a medium sized vehicle with four-wheel drive. She removes the light camouflage of tree limbs that are concealing it, and then begins her drive out of the woods, and into civilization.

* * *

Julia drives along the blacktop road and spots a gas station sign off in the distance. She sees the highway running beside it. She has her bearings now and knows exactly where she is.

Her dad took her camping around the area when she was young. She looks down at her fuel gauge, full, but she still feels the urge to stop. She pulls over on the side of the road and contemplates it.

I'm just going to get a coffee, that's not instant for once, she says to herself. And a sandwich with some fresh meat, that's not from a can. I won't talk to anyone. I will just go in, get what I need and pay, just as I would have to do for gas anyways. Julia waits for the one car to leave the parking lot and then she makes her move. It is just a little mom-and-pop style country mart, but Julia feels like she has entered a luxurious department store. Her eyes sparkle from all of the colors of shiny cans of soda, glistening behind the glass doors. Her lips smack at all of the available selections of chips, candy, and chocolates. Her one coffee and sandwich quickly turn into a small smorgasbord. She doesn't see a clerk anywhere, but she does spot a payphone in the hall, near the restroom. She unloads her hands and begins to search for coins in Mr. Roark's wallet. She dials and waits. A boy answers.

"Hello? Hello?"

Julia begins to tear up as she hears Brian's voice. She looks up, feeling so happy, and then notices a game warden pulling up and entering the store.

"Hello…"

She slowly hangs up the phone before saying anything to Brian, before telling him that she is alive. The clerk comes back to the counter from the back office and exchanges greetings with the game warden as he enters. He makes his way toward Julia. She slowly picks up her items from the table beside the phone and walks toward the clerk, avoiding eye contact with the warden as they pass each other.

"Is this it, ma'am?"

Julia nods her head, pays the clerk, and quickly exits the store before the warden comes out of the restroom. She gets on the highway and follows the directions to Dave Sweeney's house.

All along the ride, Julia feels the effects of culture shock, after being isolated for so long. Everything looks so much bigger and much more colorful than she remembers. The trees. The buildings. The people. Everything looks different, but it gives her some sense of peace after seeing it all again.

She passes a billboard sign, advertising a news radio station. She flips the dial on the stereo. There's a commercial ad for a social media network playing, and then a broadcaster comes on.

- Welcome back to American News Network. And before we continue our scheduled program, we would just like to remind all of the listeners that haven't received their flu shots to please dial 1-800-FLU-SHOT. Or you can visit our social media page to locate the nearest AGI sponsored facility in order to receive your free, annual shot. Remember folks, regardless of what healthcare you have or if you don't have any, as of last year free flu shots are being offered to everyone. Okay, Mr. Hardy, welcome back to our show, sir. And thank you for stopping by for an interview. Michael Hardy, Senior, is the founder and President of American Global Incorporated and also the owner of our news network. Now Mr. Hardy, before we took a break we were discussing all of the charitable events that AGI was involved in. For instance, AGI has been distributing free vaccinations and health examinations to underdeveloped countries, as well as to all of the homeless shelters across America.

Thank you, Tom. Our vision at American Global Incorporated is to provide for those who can't provide for themselves, in these hard, economic times. Our number one priority is helping to keep people healthy, in order to live a more productive life. What's the point of saving this planet if we don't keep the people living here healthy enough to enjoy it? We believe very strongly that everyone should be entitled to receive common immunizations and routine examinations, regardless of their income or healthcare plan. I would personally like to thank all of the congress and politicians who have supported our initiative, and for passing the most recent healthcare law, allowing AGI to be at the forefront of the next generation of healthcare. We have the very best medical professionals and scientists at AGI, working tirelessly on developing new vaccines to counter the latest and most common viruses.

Thank you, Mr. Hardy, for stopping by and taking the time to do this interview. And thank you, to all of the listeners of ANN, for tuning in to this week's live broadcast. Join us next week, as we interview the President of South Korea and discuss their development of a new AGI research facility, as part of the new United Nations Healthcare Resolution. Stay tuned for your local news updates, coming up right after this small commercial break. -

Julia turns off the radio and tries to focus on something other than what she just heard, and what Mr. Roark had told her about the virus.

She turns off the highway and on to a dirt road, past mile marker seventy. She notices a reflection in a tree about three miles down the dirt road. She slows down the vehicle and tries to make out the object. It appears to be a small camera. A few minutes later, the dirt road ends and she gets out of the vehicle. Julia pulls out her compass, and the note with directions from Mr. Roark. She plots her course and begins walking through the woods.

About thirty minutes later, she sees the outline of a small, barn-like structure. She reaches behind her, thumbs the safety off the handgun tucked in her pants, and begins to walk toward the building, slow and steady.

* * *

"Stop right there. Put your hands on top of your head." A man's voice says from behind her.

"Please don't shoot, Mr. Sweeney, I'm…" Julia hears a branch crack behind her and then feels a barrel push slowly into her upper back.

"Put your hands, on top of your head, and get down on your knees. I won't ask again."

"Okay, please don't shoot me, Mr. Sweeney."

Julia gets down on her knees and places her hands, now somewhat shaking, on top of her head.

The man moves in and begins searching her with one hand. He pulls the handgun from her pants and puts it in his. He pulls the wallet from her jacket pocket and tosses it on the ground behind him. Satisfied with his search, he backs up with the rifle still aiming at Julia.

"How do you know my name? How did you find me?"

"I'm Julia, Julia Rawlings."

Mr. Sweeney lowers the weapon, and then raises it again.

"Prove it."

"Look in the wallet. It belongs to Mr. Roark. I'm here to ask you to help him. He's very sick and won't go to a hospital."

He bends down and opens the wallet. He sees a picture of Mr. Roark, his retired military identification card. He lowers the weapon again.

"Julia Rawlings?"

He walks around and stands in front of her. He takes off her hat and sunglasses, and then helps her stand up. He looks past her now somewhat shorter, dark brown hair, and thinner, but still healthy figure.

Her face still looked very much the same, strong but not overpowering cheek bones, her nose and lips almost perfectly symmetrical, as if they were drawn on. And her eyes, he remembered those soothing, deep hazel eyes.

Julia's nerves ease as she looks at him, knowing he recognizes her now.

"It's been years since I've seen you. Why didn't I get a message from your dad about this? I could have killed you, you know?"

Julia brushes off her knees after getting up.

"My dad doesn't know I'm here. We don't really have a way to contact him. He only calls us, when he chooses to."

"Look, I'm sorry to hear about Roark, I really am. Tommy is a good guy, but he's got cancer, he's going to die. I mean, I was just a team medic. I'm not a certified doctor or anything. The only thing I'll be able to do is help ease the pain, maybe prolong it a little bit by increasing his vitamin intake and stabilizing his immune system. I've got a family here to protect Julia." He says, looking back toward the building in the woods.

"Mr. Sweeney, I understand that, I do, but Mr. Roark needs your help. He doesn't have any family. And I know how close all of you guys were when you were in the military. You can't turn your back on him now, when he needs you the most. He's still your family too."

He thinks for a moment about what she said, and he knows she is right.

"Well, let's go inside for a minute. I've got to get some of my things first, if I'm going to do this."

He places the handgun back on safe and returns it to Julia. She places it back in the seat of her pants. They move toward the building that is concealed by camouflage netting and tree brush in the middle of the woods. As they get closer, a woman opens the makeshift door, holding a small child in one arm and a shotgun draped by her side in the other.

"Amy, this is Julia, Robert's daughter. Julia, this is my wife, Amy, and our daughter, Samantha."

The young woman places the shotgun back inside and secures the child with two arms, and then stares questionably at Julia. Dave kisses his wife on the cheek and takes the baby from her arms.

"Come inside while we get our stuff."

His wife looks at him, then at Julia, and quickly follows him to the back of the building. Julia closes the door and stands by it, looking around inside the building, obviously built by hand.

Sheets of metal were hung on the walls, appearing to be a homemade attempt at bullet resistance protection. There was one bed in the corner where the couple was now standing and talking quietly, as to not let Julia hear their conversation. The few pieces of furniture appeared to be homemade and the floor was covered with random pieces of different colored carpeting.

Julia looks at a wooden baby crib padded with blankets and thinks about how hard it must be to take care of baby, in such primitive conditions.

The couple returns after their quiet conversation with a couple of bags in hand.

"Okay, we're ready. I think it's better if we all take your car, it will look less suspicious. That, and I'm really not sure if ours would make it that far."

"We?" Julia asks. "Are you sure that's a good idea?"

"Well I'm not leaving them here alone," he fires back in a mild tone. "I don't know what I'm walking into here. None of this was planned and I'm not leaving Amy and my daughter here to fend for themselves, if I don't make it back."

"Yeah, of course. I'm sorry, Mr. Sweeney."

"Good, and you can call me Dave."

They all make their way back to the SUV and begin their trip back to the cabin.

Julia turns on the stereo to break up the awkward silence, but Dave quickly turns it off.

"I'd rather not listen to that propaganda right now."

He looks over at Julia and can see she is tired. He begins a conversation to help keep her awake for a bit. He talks about her dad and how he warned most of the team about the TSOMBIE program, before the shots started last year.

Julia wants to ask more questions along the drive, but she holds back, knowing it isn't really the right time. There is a little small talk, but there is mainly silence for most of the ride back. But it is enough to keep Julia awake, and it gives her more information to wonder about silently. And she is used to that.

Julia makes the last turn, on to the paved blacktop road, leading to the trail near the cabin.

"We're getting close," Julia says, as she looks in the rearview at Amy.

Amy appeared to be somewhat younger than Dave, but they seemed to really match each other. Both had dirty blonde hair, blue-green eyes, similar facial structures, and they were similar in their small heights with light builds. Amy was more attractive than Dave, but they looked good as a couple. Amy had been silent for the entire ride, other than some light conversation to Dave and soothing words to the baby, as if she was deep in thought.

All of them were really wondering about the same thing along the ride back, about the outside world, as they passed homes, buildings and other cars on the road. All of them were wondering how everything that appeared to be so normal-looking was now somehow, all different.

* * *

Julia eases off the accelerator as they come to the dead end of the blacktop road. Julia and Dave look at each other with caution, and then back at the truck parked at the dead end. It has a decal of 'Trigg County Game Warden' across the tailgate.

"What do we do?" Julia asks Dave, with tension in her voice.

"Slow down and pull over on the side of the road."

They sit there for a moment, observing, and see that nobody is in the truck.

"What are we going to do? She asks again.

"We wait for him to come out. I'll take care of it." Dave replies as he gets out of the vehicle, opening the rear hatch.

Dave takes out the bags and finds a tire iron and spare tire under the floor board. He props the spare tire against the front fender, and then lets some of the air out of the tire on the vehicle.

Julia lowers the window and whispers to him, "Now what?"

"We wait," he says calmly.

"What if he found the cabin? What if he found Mr. Roark? We should go to the cabin."

"No, he's probably just doing routine hunting area checks. He's a game warden, that's what they do. Anyways, he could be close by, watching us right now. If we go down to the cabin then he could see us, and then he could either follow us or call it in. We wait."

Dave makes a slow attempt at changing the tire, in the event they are being watched by the warden.

About half an hour later, Dave hears leaves rustling and sees some brush moving.

"Alright, if he asks any questions, we say that we got lost going to a family reunion for the holidays and caught a flat. We are just trying to change it and get back on the road."

"Hey there," the warden says, as he approaches them from a distance.

"Hi." Dave stands up slowly, trying to block open view inside the vehicle.

"Talk about bad luck. We got a little lost and then had a tire go out on us. We are just going to change it here and be on our way."

The warden looks around Dave and in the car at Julia, and then peers in the backseat. He stares briefly at Amy and the baby, both looking back at him.

"Where you headed?"

"The camp grounds," Dave replies.

"Yeah, you're a little turned around then. You need to go back out to the gas station and turn left. Where you folks coming in from?"

The warden is now looking back at Julia, with a blank expression on his face.

"Bowling Green," Dave says. The warden walks around the vehicle as if he's checking to see if anything else is wrong, pausing briefly at the license plate, and then comes back around to Dave.

"Well, we're just as friendly here in Tennessee. Let me put my rifle up and I'll give you a hand."

"Thanks, but you really don't have to. I don't want to bother you. Really, I can fix it myself."

"It's no problem, I'm glad to help."

The warden starts walking back to his truck and Dave looks at Julia, and then his wife.

The warden returns a few minutes later and bends down at the front tire.

"Yeah, I was watching you for about ten or fifteen minutes before I came over, watching you trying to get the tire off. It looked like you needed some help. Ladies, I'm going need you to step out for a minute before I can raise the vehicle."

They get out slowly and move to the side of the road.

"So, the first thing you do is get a good flat spot on the ground, and then find a lift point on the car. Here we go. Then, you loosen all of the lug nuts while it's still on the ground. Looks like you only got two more to take off here."

He loosens the last two lug nuts.

"There we go. Now we raise it up."

He jacks the tire off the ground and lays the tire iron behind him, at Dave's foot. Dave bends down and picks up the tire iron and draws it back slowly. Julia and his wife's eyes open wide and then they turn away, closing them.

Ding, Ding...Ding, Ding. A phone in the warden's pocket begins to make noise. Dave quickly lowers the tire iron back down, beside his leg.

The warden stands up and pulls his phone from his coat. He scrolls through his social media messages and then looks at Dave. And then, with no expression and without saying anything, he starts walking back to his truck. Dave looks at Julia shaking her head, but he starts following the warden anyway.

"Sir, sir. Hey, where are you going?"

The warden doesn't reply. He gets in his truck. Dave smacks the window.

"Hey, stop! Where are you going?"

The warden buckles his seatbelt, starts the truck, and begins to pull off. Dave hits the door of his truck several times.

"Stop! Wait!"

Dave chases him, running alongside the truck until he arrives back at their car. And then he stops and watches the truck drive out of their sight. Julia and Amy come over to his side.

Dave looks at them. "What the hell just happened?"

"Let's just go," Amy says nervously.

Dave starts putting the tire back on, fast. After he secures the tire, they drive down the trail and park the SUV in the woods. They get everything out of the vehicle and then attempt to camouflage it with the pile of brush lying on the ground beside it. Julia points them in the direction of the cabin and they start walking.

"Do you think he's coming back?" Julia asks.

"I don't think so. He must have received a message sent from The Society. He definitely acted weird after he read the message, like a zombie or something. I'm not exactly sure how the memory works in their messaging, like when it comes to remembering what happened before receiving a message. But I think we are okay."

Dave really doesn't know if he is right, but he doesn't want his wife or Julia to panic.

"We'll ask Tommy when we get to the cabin. He's more read in on the TSOMBIE program than me."

Julia agrees without saying anything and they continue their small trek through the forest. And again, they remain mostly silent, keeping their concerns and thoughts to themselves.

* * *

Julia opens the door and immediately goes to check on Mr. Roark. She kneels down beside the couch and gently places her hand on Mr. Roark's shoulder, covered by the blanket.

"Mr. Roark, Mr. Roark."

She gently pushes his shoulder, with no response back. She looks back at Dave, now hovering right behind her.

"Mr. Roark..." She falls back against Dave's leg as Mr. Roark lets outs several loud, growling coughs.

He turns over and removes the blanket from his face. His eyes squint as they gain focus on the figures standing behind Julia.

"Sweeney? Is that you?" He coughs a few more times as he smiles in between the gasps for air.

"Tommy, why didn't you contact me sooner?"

Mr. Roark tries to sit up and Dave helps him.

"Julia, can you grab me some water and a towel for him?

Dave balls up the stained towel lying beside Mr. Roark. Then he unzips his small duffle bag and pulls out a stethoscope and several bottles of pills, mainly vitamins and pain relievers.

Julia returns with the water and towel.

Dave opens a few of the bottles, separates the pills, and then places them in Mr. Roark's hand.

"Take these," Dave says, as he wipes some of the blood from Mr. Roark's face.

Julia turns to Dave's wife and points her in the direction of the bedroom.

"There's a bed and bathroom down the hall if you need to rest."

Dave looks at his wife, "I'll be out here if you need me. Go get some rest honey."

Mr. Roark swallows the pills and lets out a few more coughs after he drinks the water. He looks at Dave's wife walking down the hall and then back at Dave with raised eyebrows.

"We didn't plan it okay..." Dave pauses as he begins adjusting the stethoscope, "...it just happened."

"What? I didn't say anything."

Dave gives him a quick glare and then bends him forward, placing the chest piece on Mr. Roark's upper back.

"I just wish I could land a gorgeous girl like that, younger than me." Mr. Roark says and laughs a little, while winking at Julia.

Dave quickly removes the earpiece, "Damn it, Tommy! I didn't come all the way down here, leave my peaceful safe-house, and risk almost getting caught by a game warden, just to hear you crack jokes."

He places the earpiece back in and repositions the chest piece, a little lower on Mr. Roark's back.

"What game warden?" Mr. Roark asks seriously now.

Dave removes the earpiece again and looks at Julia.

"It's nothing, there was a game warden doing some routine trail checks nearby, and then he left. There's nothing to worry about. He was in the woods opposite of the direction of the cabin, we're fine."

Mr. Roark looks to Julia for her reassurance.

She pauses and then nods in concurrence with Dave's remarks.

Mr. Roark believes her and bends back forward for Dave to continue his exam.

Dave looks at Julia with an expression of thanks and places the earpiece back in, continuing his exam on Mr. Roark.

"Julia, why don't you extend some hospitality to Mrs. Sweeney there and see if she would like some of our finest whiskey?"

Dave nods his head in approval.

Mr. Roark looks at Julia and winks again.

"If she's over twenty-one of course," Mr. Roark says as he lets out a big laugh, followed by a loud cough.

"Seriously!" Dave yanks the earpiece back out.

"You just couldn't resist, could you?" Dave barks back.

Julia joins in with Mr. Roark laughing and then Dave looks at both of them, and then he begins to laugh a little too.

Mr. Roark gives Dave a hug.

"I'm really glad to see you brother, it means a lot to me for you to risk everything and come here. I mean that."

Julia returns with some glasses and a fresh bottle of whiskey, and then goes to the bedroom with a glass for Amy. Julia sits it down beside her on the night stand and gently shuts the door, not to wake the baby.

Amy picks up the glass and whispers, "Thank you."

Julia closes the door and rejoins the two in the living room, interrupting their small talk with her glass.

"A toast. A toast to old friendships, and the beginning of new ones."

Julia smiles at Mr. Roark and then to Dave. They all take their shots and let out small sighs. Then they all take seats by the fireplace and Julia places some fresh wood on the fire that is almost out.

Mr. Roark looks at Dave and then back at Julia.

"Your dad called while you were gone, Julia. I didn't tell him that I let you go get help."

Julia pauses and then strikes another match, lighting the already kindling layer of wood, as if she doesn't care about her dad calling.

"I told him you were ready, Julia. That you are ready to leave. That you were ready to see him and begin your new identity."

Julia stands and looks at Dave, then at him.

"What about you? I can't just leave you here."

"I'll take care of him, Julia. That's why I came. I'll see this through."

She looks at Mr. Roark again, as he stands and walks over to her.

"You are the strongest and smartest person that I have ever known, Julia. You always amazed me, even when you were little. You're ready. Now that Dave's here, you can go where you're really needed."

He gently kisses her on the forehead.

"How? How am I going to get there? Am I going to drive the whole way, wherever that is? Or is he coming here?"

"I'll go over all the details with you tomorrow. You get some rest now, Julia. You've done more than enough today."

Julia looks at Dave and then gives Mr. Roark a gentle hug.

"Okay. Goodnight."

Julia goes to the back bedroom, opposite of Amy, and begins closing the door slowly while peeking through the gap just before it closes. She takes a long look at the two of them talking but she can't make out what they're saying. She looks at Mr. Roark, smiling and laughing with Dave. She relaxes at his appearance and the fact that someone else is here to help. She smiles, and then closes the remaining gap in the door.

SIXTEEN

Captain Brown shuts off his computer and looks out his window, down at the formation of Soldiers. They are all receiving their flu shots by the medical unit. He packs his briefcase and looks at his watch, four p.m. He closes the blinds and leaves his office.

"Have a good night, sir."

"Thanks, Sergeant Jones, you too."

"Sir, just a reminder, you and the remaining leadership within the unit have flu shots scheduled for zero-nine-hundred hours tomorrow morning. That will make bring us to one-hundred percent sir."

Justin hesitates at the door and then silently acknowledges the comment before he exits.

He exits the military base, passing several formations of troops in fields and open hangars, all receiving flu shots and exams. He pauses at the highway intersection and switches his left turn signal on, instead of the normal right he would take to go home. He pulls out his personal phone and begins sending a text to his wife.

- sorry baby, late night flight,
b home late, luv u -

Justin waits for a reply text message for a few seconds, and then a car beeps their horn behind him. He puts the phone down and makes the left turn. He exits the highway after driving for almost an hour and pulls into a shopping mall parking lot, and he waits. He sits waiting and watching all of the people coming and going, shopping. All appears normal, but Justin feels sick to his stomach from thinking of everything Dr. Singer had told him. He couldn't stop imagining all of those people slowly losing control of their lives without ever knowing it, without ever knowing that the world was changing, right before them.

* * *

A late model sedan pulls in behind him and rolls down the tinted window. He sees that it's Dr. Singer and he gets in his car with him. They begin driving out of the city.

"So…where are we going?"

Dr. Singer lights a cigarette and cracks his window.

"To my house."

Justin glances over at him with a somewhat surprised look on his face, not expecting to hear his house as an answer.

They continue the ride in silence and pull into an obviously rich, residential neighborhood, with nice houses and expensive cars. They pull into a driveway at the end of the neighborhood. Dr. Singer opens the gate with a remote inside the car and drives into the garage at the back of the house. A truck and another sedan are parked in the back of the house as well. Justin isn't sure if they are Dr. Singer's or if he should expect someone else to be there.

Dr. Singer gets out of the car as Justin sits there quietly for a moment, still surprised he is at his house.

This is definitely not where Justin pictured him, this paranoid man, of living. When he told Justin that they were going to his house, thoughts of some isolated shack or farm on the edge of society raced through Justin's mind, not anything normal like this.

He gets out and follows behind Dr. Singer to the door.

"Nice House."

Dr. Singer looks back at him as he opens the door, knowing this is not what Captain Brown had imagined.

"Part of the game, the art of infiltrating, is to blend in. You probably thought I lived in a cave somewhere, didn't you?"

"No, not at all. Well, maybe a little."

Justin follows Dr. Singer through the house, taking notice of the nice decorations. They appear to be suitable for a wealthy doctor's salary. Dr. Singer stops at the kitchen and starts separating bottles of alcohol in his cabinets as if he's looking for a particular bottle. Justin walks over to a small table and picks up a photo of a young beautiful woman with Dr. Singer, obviously from decades earlier as the doctor appeared to be Justin's age in the photo. He hears the cabinet close and puts down the photo quickly, trying not to be noticed by Dr. Singer. Dr. Singer starts walking toward the hallway and motions for Justin to follow him. They get to the end of the hallway and enter into a large bathroom. He hands the bottle to Justin and starts un-tucking his shirt.

"Um, okay, I'm going to be right outside."

Dr. Singer gives him a sharp look and then opens the cabinet under the sink. He gets down on a knee and reaches deep under the sink, and after a few seconds a very loud metallic click comes from the tub area. Justin raises his eyebrows in question. Dr. Singer goes over to the tub, where the loud click came from, and reaches around the edge of it with both hands as if he's going to pull it. The tub slowly begins to slide out from the wall while Dr. Singer steps backwards, pulling it with a steady pace. He stops pulling and a stairwell to a basement is exposed.

Now that is more like the Dr. Singer I know, Justin thinks to himself.

"Watch your step, Justin."

Justin trails behind Dr. Singer down the homemade stairs and into a large, sophisticated room of computers, television screens, and maps. There are charts and link diagrams with several names and different photos of people. Social media pages are displayed on several computer screens and

'American News Network' is broadcasting on multiple televisions.

Justin is taken back at how elaborate of a setup he had. But the small operations center definitely matched with Dr. Singer's style and personality. He scans over to Dr. Singer, who is already bent over top of a computer, typing rapidly.

"Bring that bottle over here, would you?"

Justin snaps out of his temporary daze.

"This is a pretty big setup here. You did it all yourself?"

Dr. Singer takes the bottle and just looks at him. He begins pouring two glasses, without answering his question.

"Right."

Justin takes his glass and walks over to the large white board area that is pasted full of diagrams, photos, and news clippings.

'The Society' is written at the top center of the large board, with 'American Global Inc.' written just below it. There are several famous world events that are pasted on the board, most of which Justin remembers, or at least knows about. There are several terrorist incidents and flu pandemics on the timeline of events, all ultimately linking to The Society and American Global Inc. on the diagram. There is a photo of an older man underneath American Global Inc. with 'Michael Hardy Sr.' labeled on it. The diagram also has links to several, major government organizations, some of which the photos of people or names are scratched out with an

'X' over them. Justin peers in closer to one of the many names, Dr. William Nichols.

"Is this the doctor you were telling me about before? Dr. Nichols?"

Dr. Singer types a few more keys on the computer and then walks over to Justin with the bottle of whiskey. Dr. Singer pours himself another glass. He swallows the drink quickly and then lights a cigarette. He refills Justin's glass that still has most of the first round in it.

"Yeah, that's the same doctor." Dr. Singer replies as he walks over to another computer and pulls up some websites on a television screen. He rolls out another board with a map of the United States on it. The map has thumbtacks in different states. A few names and numbers are written on it as well. It is a replica of the same map and names that Dr. Singer keeps in his office.

"These are all of the people I have as of now, to help us." He points to the locations on the map.

"Those people listed on the map there are not infected. A few are permanently immune, but most have simply avoided the vaccinations and are 'underground' so to speak."

Justin looks over the small list of names that are under written under the 'Permanently Immune' section. He sees 'Julia Rawlings' with 'Dr. Erika Gordon' written under it. He thinks that she might be Dr. Singer's daughter, based on the similarities in appearance and the fact her photos are bigger than the others, and appearing to be organized with more care. But they have different last names, his name is

Singer. Then his focus quickly shifts as he notices his name on the list, with 'AGI Corporate Pilot' written below and then scratched out with 'AGI Analyst' written over top. He wants to ask about why he was under that list, but he wants to know what the other remarks meant first.

"What is this? I'm not a corporate pilot or an analyst. Wait, is this your plan for me? You want me to work for this organization that is supposedly responsible for...for taking over the world basically? I'm just a military pilot man, I'm not special operations like you were. I mean I'm not trained for this type of thing. I know I told you I was in and I would help, but this seems, I don't know, not realistic."

Justin puts down his glass and takes a seat. He hangs his head in doubt, thinking that maybe he is in over his head, thinking maybe he should have never came here after all.

"That woman you saw in the photo upstairs, that was my second wife."

Dr. Singer takes a seat and lights another cigarette. Justin stops worrying for a moment and focuses on Dr. Singer.

"I was relatively young when I started my cover life as Dr. Singer, roughly around your age, in my twenties. At the time she was just a piece of the puzzle in the bigger scheme of things. But, I grew to love this woman, just as much as my first wife, from my original life as Robert Rawlings. I had no intentions of having a family with this cover wife, it wouldn't be fair to do that to her, or my real wife.

But in any case, we did, we had a child. There were complications during the pregnancy, and she died during an emergency induced labor. I was burdened with a lot of grief and anxiety about the whole thing. I couldn't manage taking care of a baby in my cover life, alone, while maintaining my real life with two kids and first wife in the other. I wasn't much a father figure type anyway. So, I gave the baby up for adoption and continued my two lives, a widowed doctor in one, and a married, father of two in the other. That was the toughest obstacle in my life that I ever had to overcome. It was tougher than any military operation I had done. But I made it through it."

Justin sits there quietly and looks at the man who he had known for so long, and up to this point as, Dr. Singer. Robert Rawlings, Justin thinks to himself. Finally. And Julia 'Rawlings' from the board, I knew that had to be his daughter. Justin is relieved to finally know his real name. It puts him at ease. He wants to continue the conversation and find out more.

"What happened to the kid, the one you gave up?"

"My point of the story, Justin, is that you can do the impossible, even when facing impossible odds, as long as you never quit. Quitting is the easy choice, the easy way out."

Justin takes another drink and sits in deep thought for a few seconds, focusing on another question that might not be as sensitive as the one Dr. Singer just ignored.

"So, permanently immune? How do you know I am permanently immune? My name is on your list over there. How do you know anyone on that list is permanently immune for that matter? And if you know so much, then why can't you just create the anti-virus yourself and give it to everyone? If this virus has been developed that much over the years, and you and Dr. Nichols have been studying it that long, you should have an anti-virus of your own by now, right?"

"The Society keeps the permanent immune formula extremely close-hold, within their top leadership only. I told you that before. Even with our combined years of research, we still don't know everything about the program due to the extreme security of The Society. If they weren't good at what they did then we probably wouldn't be having this conversation right now Justin. Even Dr. Nichols is limited to what he has access to, and he is their head laboratory director. Only the top leaders, within their 'Inner Circle' have full access and knowledge of how everything about the virus works. It really wasn't until Phase One was released that we were able to better understand how the immunity worked. Unfortunately, the diaries of our forefathers, who were involved in the original World War One experiments, did not have the data for the anti-virus that they injected themselves with. We know they tried to recreate it but couldn't. There were just so many steps and chemicals involved and without all of them working on it in the same place, it was just too much for them to do individually. And they were watched extremely close after the war was over."

Robert and Justin both take a drink.

"We, me and Dr. Nichols, tried to replicate the anti-TSOMBIE vaccine over the years as well. But until we had our hands on the actual Phase One virus, we were just guessing at the exact vaccine makeup that we were using to create the anti-virus. We would think we were getting close and then another pandemic would breakout. Then we would find out that their virus was being altered, perfected every time they tested it on a large scale. But when Phase One was initiated, even if we had an anti-virus, it was already too late. We have always been several steps behind them. But a couple of months ago, when Dr. Nichols ran the tests on his son, we learned the invaluable secret about the anti-virus being hereditary, like I told you before. What I didn't tell you was that we both injected ourselves with the TSOMBIE virus too, and nothing happened. It was just a theory after his son, so we had to know for sure, we had to. There are only two ways to become permanently immune. The first way being to receive the anti-virus, which is too late now for anyone that has already received Phase One. And the second way is to be born with the immune DNA."

"So, what about me? I was born with it, right?"

"I've researched the couple that adopted you and they are not members of The Society. So yes, you were born with immune DNA."

Justin plops back in the sofa and looks up at the ceiling for a moment. Robert lights another cigarette and looks at him, thinking about what to tell him next. Thinking about whether he should tell him more, should he tell him more upsetting facts about his life?

"My parents never told me I was adopted you know. After you told me that night at the bar, I went home and went back through all of the paperwork I had from them. I researched all of the court records, all of the records I could find, and there was nothing ever showing an adoption for me. I need to see some type of proof that what you're telling me here is the truth Dr. Singer. Robert. I'm not sure what to call you by now, but that's beside the point. So after not finding records about an adoption, I thought about the memories I had growing up. And I remembered that I was never really anything like my parents. I didn't act like them and I definitely didn't look like them, so it's not beyond the realm of possibilities that I was adopted. But I'm still going to need more than just your word. Sorry."

Robert goes over to a cabinet. He pulls out a folder and hands it to Justin.

"What you're about to see is going to be hard on you, and you may get upset, but you deserve to know the truth, the entire truth. And as far as the name goes, well I'll let you decide on what you want to call me, after you read what's in that folder."

Robert pours himself another glass and leaves the bottle with Justin. He walks out of the basement and up the stairs, looking back at him, leaving Justin by himself.

* * *

Justin sits quietly, staring at the folders in front of him, wondering what's in them. He pours himself a drink. Slowly, he opens the folder and begins skimming through a hospital report a few pages in.

- *...Amanda Singer, Mother...due to unseen complications during surgery...Bill Singer, Father....Joshua Singer, child...born in good health and then was placed...* -

"Wait a minute, what?" Justin stops for a moment and then continues reading, aloud this time. "Bill Singer, Father. Occupation, Doctor at St. Mary's Hospital?" He looks back up the stairs and then back at the folder. He continues flipping through the documents. He stops at a non-disclosure adoption agreement.

- ...Father Bill Singer is hereby relinquishing all parental rights of said child to the full care and custody of Paul and Samantha Brown... -

Justin stops reading and puts the folder down. He takes a few moments to gather his composure and comprehend it all. He tries to comprehend that everything he had grown up believing about his parents, his life, was a lie. His blood pressure begins to boil, thinking about Dr. Singer, Robert Rawlings, and all of his secrets and lies. Why didn't he tell me this when we first met? Why didn't my parents ever tell me? Justin repeatedly asks himself these questions over and over again in his head. He tries to fill in the answers from what Dr. Singer had already told him. He finishes his glass of whiskey and now he just wanted to go home, anywhere to get away from him, this man.

This man, who was once just a man to Captain Brown, was now much more.

* * *

Justin goes upstairs and finds Dr. Singer sitting in a chair. He walks past him to the garage door and looks back, "Take me to my car. Now please."

Robert thinks about how Justin must feel.

He hated letting him find out, but in order for Justin to be able to do what Robert needed him to, then they would have to trust each other. The only way Robert knew how to completely earn his trust was to let him know the truth, regardless of how painful it was.

Robert drives Justin back to the parking lot, the same way they drove to the house, in silence. This is a different type of silence though. The anxiety and eagerness is now shifted to Robert, as he wonders if Justin would still help him. He knows better than to ask him any questions, he could tell Justin is upset, and rightfully so.

They pull into the parking lot and Justin exits without saying a word and walks to his car. He pauses at the door and walks back to Robert's car. Robert rolls the window down, waiting for Justin to punch him or spit in his face.

"I'm not going to go back on my word, of helping you do this. But let's get one thing straight, from this point forward, no more secrets, no more lies! You tell me everything and you answer all of my questions from now on. Clear?"

"Okay. Okay, Justin."

Justin, now feeling a small sense of gratification and confidence, asks him a question.

"Now, is there anything, anything else you need to tell me?"

Robert answers, knowing he couldn't afford anything other than telling Justin the clear facts from this point forward.

"You have a sister, and a brother, from my first wife."

"No kidding?" Justin says with full sarcasm in his voice. "I was kind of able to put that one together myself there, Mr. Obvious."

They both just look at each other, with somewhat less tension now.

"So, what's next then?"

"I'll draw up the medical paperwork recommending your discharge from the military and then we start your training to become an AGI analyst, immediately. I'll call you tomorrow with more details and we'll work out a schedule for your training, at my house. I know you don't want to hear my recommendation about leaving your wife now, before it gets worse, but…"

Justin cuts him off, "Let's just take it one step at a time okay. Try and remember that some people still have normal relationships, normal relationships with their family…Robert."

Robert sits quietly as Justin walks back to his car. They both drive away from the empty parking lot alone, and anxious, anxious about their future relationship together.

SEVENTEEN

Mike Hardy looks up from his computer to the knocking at his glass office door. He waves his young assistant in and turns around to pour himself the last cup of coffee for the day.

"Good evening, sir. I wanted to brief you on some updates before you went home."

The assistant hands Hardy a folder, labeled with 'International Situation Report Update.' Then he walks to the flat-screen television on the wall and plugs in a USB flash drive. He flips through the folders and images and pulls up a map of Mexico and South America, labeled 'Operation Village Sweep.'

"Sir, we're about seventy-five percent complete with Operation Village Sweep and still on target to be complete before Phase Three begins. The ones that are not healthy enough to build the wall are being labeled as casualties of drug and gang violence, or illegal border crossers. This includes a variety of death types we are using, such as accidental deaths, dehydration, and use of deadly force by our law enforcement officers."

The analyst then flips to another map, of Asia. Korea is highlighted.

"Sir, the statistics are still leaning toward dissolving North Korea. The majority of our surveillance still shows that the government is refusing to administer the shots as directed. Course of action number two would be to replace more leaders of their government with three additional Society members. But, the underdeveloped population and low economic status still remains of very little value to us. It's more profitable and sustainable to relocate and repurpose the population. This would allow more geographical areas for Society members to establish their own communities and resorts. The land itself remains the only thing of real value to us at this point sir."

He turns off the television and hands Hardy another folder, labeled with 'Operation BL 2020.' Hardy takes a drink of coffee as he opens the folder and begins reading over the files.

"Continue. I'm listening."

"Based off your previous guidance sir, we have begun increased targeting and surveillance on all non-Society, bloodline individuals. We are only about a quarter of the way through all of their second party contacts, and no increase on third party contacts yet. And that's not including the two additional non-Society bloodlines that we are still working on."

"What's the issue, Chris? You know this a priority now."

"We are still understaffed, sir. We are hiring more analysts, but, well it's the screening process that's causing the delay, sir. We have to wait until the blood work comes back from the lab on all new employees before they start working. And that takes a while, based on what the lab is telling me, sir."

Hardy looks up from the folder and then at his assistant, with a serious and concerned look in his eyes.

"I can make it work with the analysts we have now sir, but it will simply take more time. Phase Three analysts just don't function as fast as uninfected employees. They can literally work twenty-four hours straight, but they are just not as fast due to the somewhat slower motor functions caused by the virus."

"Alright. Enough, I got it. Set up an office call with Dr. Nichols."

"Yes, sir."

"No forget it, I'll call him tomorrow myself and find out what the delay is, and how we can speed up the hiring process. I can't afford to brief the old man on any more delays or setbacks."

"Yes, sir."

He hands Hardy another folder, labeled with 'Pending Approval for Release to Network and Communications.'

"These are pending your approval sir, as you directed. It's just the normal significant activities we were tracking plus the intelligence summary updates, only on the twenty-three internal Society bloodlines. There are no second party contact intelligence summaries ready to be released yet."

Hardy thumbs through each of the pages, scanning them over and initialing at the bottom of each one. He closes the folder and signs the release form, 'Approved for Release to Network and Communications.' Hardy stands up and puts on his coat. He begins closing out the open files on his computer and picks up the folders on his desk.

"Any updates on the other thing we talked about?"

"No, sir. We haven't picked up on any new or unusual messaging or broadcasts."

The analyst clears his throat as Hardy walks past him, toward his door.

"However, I have personally noticed something else sir, something that you may find interesting."

Hardy stops at the door and turns back, facing the analyst with curiosity.

"Ms. McNeil has still been at Headquarters every night after I go home. And here lately, with the new operations, that has been pretty late sir. On average I have been leaving around midnight and I've seen her driver waiting outside, every night, when I leave."

Hardy adjusts his coat. He thinks quietly for a second while holding the door open for the analyst to exit.

"Thanks, Chris. That's good to know. And great work with the updates, keep it up. I'll see you tomorrow."

"Thank you, sir. Oh, and Mr. Hardy, any update on the decision for my permanent immunity, sir?"

"Just keep performing Chris, and you have nothing to worry about. Take care of me and I'll make sure you are taken care of, that's how it works. Goodnight."

"Yes sir, thank you, sir. Goodnight."

Mike Hardy lets the analyst out and utters to himself quietly, "What are you up to Tasha?"

EIGHTEEN

Julia eases open the wooden bedroom door, trying not to wake the baby in the other room beside her. She tiptoes past the living room after using the bathroom. The fire is barely going, and the living room is noticeably colder. She looks over at Mr. Sweeney, curled up on the floor beside the dying fire. Then she glances over at Mr. Roark, buried into the couch, with his face covered as usual. She gently smiles at both of the men sleeping and a feeling of ease comes over her. She thinks about Mr. Roark being nursed back to health, and how she now has more than one person to have a conversation with.

She turns back toward the kitchen and jumps a little, startled by seeing Amy and the baby already awake and standing at the sink. Amy was pointing out the window, trying to show the baby the deer. She looks behind her to Julia, and smiles. Julia smiles back. She walks up and touches the baby's hand, "You see the deer?" Julia whispers gently. Baby Samantha, still unable to talk, responds back in baby mumble, causing Julia and Amy to laugh. Julia grabs a bottle of water and slowly exits the back door. She watches the deer from the back porch as she begins stretching, getting ready for her morning workout routine.

Julia slows her morning jog to a walk as she approaches Mr. Roark's SUV, still covered in light brush and tree limbs. She adjusts a couple of the branches and adds a few more, slightly improving the camouflage. She picks up a jog again along the firebreak. After a few minutes of light jogging again, she begins to see a break in the tree line. It is where the firebreak trail connected to the pavement. Knowing that this is as far as she needs to go, she slows her pace to a walk again and then stops. She stretches lightly, takes a few relaxing breaths, and prepares to begin her jog back.

The loud sound of a car door being shut echoes through the early morning calm of the woods, and Julia immediately crouches down. She begins creeping slowly into the densely vegetated forest, away from the open trail she was just on. She freezes once she feels somewhat concealed by the brush, and then begins scanning through the woods with her eyes. She tries to dial in on where the noise came from. "Come on, you got to be kidding me," Julia mumbles to herself as she sees it, the game warden truck, the same exact one. "No, no, no." She zooms in focus with her eyes and sees the warden getting his rifle from the back of the truck. He turns and begins to walk toward the firebreak trail. "Turn around, turn around." Julia mumbles to herself nervously. The warden stops just before reaching the trail and says something into his radio. Then he turns and starts walking back towards the truck. "That's it, keep going." Julia looks back down the trail, back towards the direction of the cabin. She plots out a new course in her head on shortening the distance and staying off the trail as much as possible. She looks back at the warden, now inside of the truck with the door open. "Here we go." Julia seizes the opportunity and makes a break for it, back to the cabin.

* * *

Breathing heavily, Julia bursts through the back door and immediately locks it. She stares hard out of the window and at the woods. Dave and his wife are standing quietly by the couch with the baby and then they both turn around to Julia's loud entrance. Julia finally turns around after scanning the woods for a few moments, catching her breath a little. She wipes her face with her shirt and begins walking toward the living room. She can sense something is off with Dave and Amy, but she can't quite put her finger on it. Amy looks like she has been crying, but the baby is fine in her arms. Dave just has an empty expression on his face. Mr. Roark? Is he…Julia cuts off her own thought. She doesn't want to imagine the possibility of it, but inside she knows, she knows what is wrong. She blocks it out.

"There's...the umm..." She is trying to tell them about the game warden. But at the same time, she is still trying to catch her breath from the long sprint back, and still battling her thoughts about Mr. Roark.

"At the firebreak...there's...we have to wake Mr. Roark, now."

She starts toward the couch and Dave puts his arm out to stop her. She smacks his arm and brushes him back. She bends down to Mr. Roark, still covered with the blanket over his face. She starts shaking his lifeless arm, now cold to the touch, even through the blanket.

Julia knew it. She knew it when she first looked at Dave's face.

"I'm sorry, Julia. He just...I woke up this morning and found him like this."

Julia lets go of his arm and wipes her face as she stands back up.

"I'm fine. I'm fine. We all knew this day was coming sooner or later."

Dave puts his arm on her shoulder and she backs away, regaining her composure.

"We should bury him and then leave." Julia says firmly, pulling the curtain to the side and then looking out of the front window. She wipes her face again, with her back turned towards them.

"Leave? And go where? Back to our last rat-hole of a home that we left? David?" Amy asks quickly and looks at Dave, who shakes his head softly, trying to keep the situation calm.

He walks over to Julia at the window.

"You saw our last home, Julia. This place is much better, especially to raise a child in. The only other option is to go to your dad. But the only person that knew where to find him was, Mr. Roark."

"You don't understand, Dave. It's not safe here anymore. That's what I was trying to tell you when I first came in. I saw the game warden again."

Julia looks back at Amy and the baby, "It's not safe here."

Dave looks at Julia and his wife, and then begins peeking out of the curtains on the front and back windows of the cabin. Amy takes a seat in the chair and sits the baby down on the floor in front of her. She begins to weep silently while looking at Julia.

"Look, I know this must be hard for both of you, but it will be safer for all of us to just leave and try to find my dad. He's obviously been preparing for whatever is happening right now, and I promise you, it will be safe wherever he is at."

Julia bends down and places her hand on Amy's shoulder.

Amy moves away from Julia's touch. She picks the baby up at her feet and places the child in her lap.

"I'm not going on some wild goose chase across the country, with a baby. Are you kidding me? No, I know what we need to do. We have to kill him. We kill the game warden and then get rid of the body, and then we'll be fine. David?" Amy looks at Dave, waiting, expecting him to side with her on this.

Dave looks back over his shoulder after the comment from his wife, and then continues looking out the window. He avoids eye contact with Julia, who is now staring at him, also waiting. Julia is waiting for a logical response to his wife's absurd comment, expecting him to side with her on this.

Julia stands up and backs away from the chair, taking his silence as siding with Amy.

"You can't be serious, Dave? We are not killing anybody, alright. How can that help us at all?"

Dave looks back again. This time he does look at Julia, but then he slowly puts his head down and breaks eye contact.

"Think about what you are saying right now. He is a game warden for crying out loud! That's the same as killing a cop!" Julia takes a breath and calms down. "All I am saying is that people are going to look for him when he goes missing, and then there could dozens of cops around here. We need to bury Mr. Roark and leave, period."

Dave goes over to his wife and stands face to face with her. He looks at Julia for a second and then straight at Amy.

"Julia's right honey, it would draw too much attention to us. We'll bury Mr. Roark, and then leave. I know some possible places to look for her father." Dave looks back at Julia. "And the sooner we get going, the better."

Amy gets upset. Upset at her husband's decision against her, she storms off to the bedroom with the baby, closing the door hard behind her.

"We need to do this fast alright, and quietly."

"Thank you, Dave."

"Don't thank me okay. I didn't save Mr. Roark. And now we're homeless, with a small child." He quietly yells to her.

He takes a moment and calms down for taking his frustration out on Julia.

"I'm sorry. I didn't mean to take it out on you, Julia. Let's just get this over with and get out of here. Wrap the blanket around him and grab that side. We'll just use that to slide him out to the woods."

Julia grabs the blanket and gets ready to lift.

"Okay, here we go. One, two…"

Dave's counting is interrupted by a loud series of knocks on the back door. Julia and Dave lock eyes, immediately knowing that it was too late, the warden had found them.

* * *

"What do you want to do?" Julia asks and waits for a response as the knocking continues, with another three loud thumps.

Amy opens the bedroom door and Dave motions for her to go back inside.

"Alright, let me think for a second."

Dave takes a moment to think about what to do, while looking at Mr. Roark and then at the back door.

"Okay, I've got something. I'll keep him outside and see if he recognizes me. We still don't know how their memory works after being infected. If he does recognize me, then I will tell him we came back to get our uncle." He looks back at Mr. Roark's body on the couch. "And he's just a little drunk right now, sleeping it off. The warden seemed pretty harmless the other day, right? I think we'll be okay. What do you think?"

Julia nods in approval of the plan and moves behind the hallway wall. She peers around the edge, watching Dave as he moves to the backdoor.

Dave opens the door and shakes hands with the warden. He quickly closes the door behind him and steps out on the porch, keeping the warden outside. Julia creeps over to the suitcase and puts her handgun in the back of her pants, preparing for the worst. She moves back behind the wall and tries to listen to their conversation, but it's too muffled. She starts moving back toward the kitchen to get within hearing distance and then Dave opens the door, with the warden walking in right behind him.

Dave looks at Julia. He tries to ease her tension with his eyes, but it doesn't help.

"Umm…Erika, this is Officer Beck, he's a game warden. He just wanted to grab some water and take a rest for a moment."

Julia tries to calm her anxiety and takes a deep breath.

"Sure, umm, absolutely. Please, please, have a seat. I'll get you some water, sir."

Julia pulls out a chair and closes the briefcase on the table. She walks to the kitchen cabinets and glances at Dave as she passes, uncertainty in both their eyes now.

The warden takes off his hat as he sits down and looks at Julia, with a semi-smile, semi-blank expression on his face.

Julia opens a bottle of water and pours it into a glass, carefully, trying to regain feeling in her hands that went numb all of a sudden. She carries the glass back to the warden with both hands.

The warden takes a long drink, almost emptying the glass, and then smiles completely at Julia and Dave.

"Thank you miss. I didn't think I was going to walk this far down but I saw a SUV on the trail. So, I kept following the trail, leading me here to this cabin. I've never been out here before."

Julia and Dave look at each other, almost holding their breath at every move and word of the game warden.

"I was pretty sure I recognized the vehicle, and then when I saw the spare tire on it, it clicked."

The warden sits quietly, as if waiting on a response. Julia and Dave remain silent and respond back with nervous smiles instead. The warden gets up and puts his hat back on, and then begins a slow, investigative walk toward the living room.

"So, how long you folks been out here?"

Julia looks at Dave with confusion, confusion at what he asked, confusion on what to do if he finds out Mr. Roark is dead.

"We just came back to get our uncle and take him to our family holiday event, the one we were trying to get to yesterday."

The warden looks back at them and then over at Mr. Roark on the couch, with a blanket still covering his face and body. He picks up the bottle of whiskey on the table beside the couch and puts it back down.

"Seems like your uncle had a little too much to drink. He appears to be out cold. Is he okay?

"Yes sir, he drinks like this all the time. We're just letting him sleep it off." Dave answers quickly.

"I see. So this is his cabin then? He is the owner and he lives way out here all by himself?" The warden asks while looking around the room and down the hallway, at the bedroom doors.

"Yes, sir." Julia responds and quickly walks over to the fireplace, blocking the hallway in an attempt to keep the warden from wandering around any further.

"Well I'm sorry to have to do this, but I need to wake him up. We're doing surveys of all property owners around here to ensure they have adequate communication devices. Cell phones, radios, televisions, things like that. This is my area and I haven't been to this cabin yet. It's not even listed on the county property records. But now that I know someone lives out here, I'm going to need him to wake up and complete a communication device survey."

"Umm...well...our uncle likes to live with the bare essentials. He doesn't really have any of those types of things. You know, a real loner-type. I can fill out the survey for him though, no problem. But why exactly do you need to know about his communication devices?" Dave asks, wishing he hadn't as soon as he said it. But his curiosity took over and he blurted the question out.

"It seems like all you guys are on the bare essentials. It's been all over the internet and social media for weeks now. American Global Incorporated is sponsoring a government approved program for communication equipment. They are giving free electronics to those who can't afford them. Free internet and cable too. It's a new program to keep everyone informed and in touch with society. I can't believe you guys haven't heard about it. I just need to wake him up and get his signature on a couple of forms, and then he'll be all set up out here."

The warden starts bending down to remove the blanket. He pauses as a young child's cry rings out from the bedroom. The warden stands back up a little startled.

"Do you need to go check on your baby?" The warden asks Julia.

Julia looks at Dave and then starts walking to the bedroom. But before she gets there, the door opens, with Amy holding the baby. Julia turns back around, facing the warden and Dave. Amy takes a few steps and stands behind Julia, at the entrance of the living room. Dave looks at Amy and sees the fear in her face, pale as she fixates on the warden, who's now hovering over Mr. Roark's dead body.

"Everything's fine baby. Officer Beck just stopped in for a moment, for some water and to drop off some forms." Dave looks back at the warden. "Sir, why don't you just leave the forms with me and I can bring them by your office, after our uncle wakes up. Or I can just sign for him."

The warden stiffens his voice, "I'm sorry sir, I've got my orders and I need to collect forms on the spot from the owner, strict protocol. I'll be out of your hair in just a minute though. Honestly, it really doesn't take that long."

The warden bends back down to Mr. Roark's lifeless body and removes the blanket from his face. Julia and Dave shake their heads softly at each other, with fear and emotion. Amy's eyes lock in on the small pistol grip, barely protruding from the seat of Julia's pants.

"He doesn't look good at all. Sir. Sir. I need you to wake up sir." The warden raises his voice after each attempt, and then places his hand on Mr. Roark's shoulder. He quickly moves his hand back and stands up.

Julia looks at Dave. Then, in slow motion and what feels like an eternity, Julia locks her eyes on the warden as she feels the handgun being pulled from her pants. She sees the warden begin to move his right hand toward the gun on his belt, and Julia closes her eyes.

Before Dave could move his feet, Amy had the warden dead in her sights, with a pistol in one hand and their baby Samantha in the other.

"No!" Dave cries in desperation, but it's too late.

Shots ring out through the cabin.

Then silence.

It was over, just like that.

Dead.

Cries begin to ring out from the baby, echoing through the light gun smoke that now filled the air.

The warden lay lifeless on the couch, atop Mr. Roark. He never even drew his gun before Amy had placed two shots in his torso and one in his head.

Dead.

Just like that, it was over.

Julia opens her eyes to the fresh spatter of blood on the couch and floor. She pulls at her ears, ringing from the three shots just fired from behind her head. Amy walks over to Dave and hands him the gun and hugs him, with the baby still crying in between both of them. Dave holds them tight and lets out a deep sigh of relief. Julia sits down on the floor beside the fireplace, in disbelief of what just happened.

After a few moments, Amy takes the baby back to the bedroom and closes the door. Dave walks over to Julia and helps her up. She wipes her face and stares at the bodies on the couch.

"I guess we're digging for two now. We better get to work."

"Julia, I'm sorry. I didn't know…"

"No. Don't be. She did what had to be done. Let's just get this done and get out of here."

NINETEEN

Dr. Nichols stares intensely at the words on his computer screen, 'Please Enter Password to Access Main Server.' Frustrated and anxious, he types in a series of numbers and letters, and then takes a breath. "Come on, come on." He gently presses enter. 'Password Incorrect - Please Enter Password to Access Main Server.' He slams his fists on the keyboard and pushes himself away from the desk. He gets up and begins pacing around his office. As he walks back to his desk, he sees Mike Hardy's assistant, his right-hand analyst, being escorted by one of his lab technicians. The analyst is being escorted toward his office. Dr. Nichols quickly turns off his computer and walks to his door to meet him.

"Dr. Nichols, good morning. My name is Chris Trendell, I believe we've met before. I'm here on behalf of Mr. Hardy, Junior. May I come in and discuss the details?"

"Umm, yeah, of course. Please, have a seat." Dr. Nichols closes the door, looking at the lab technician staring back at him with an empty expression on his face.

"Those Phase Three employees aren't much for conversation, are they? You must get pretty bored down here with such minimal, intellectual interactions?"

Dr. Nichols takes a seat behind his desk, in front of the smug analyst.

"I'm pretty tied up in research and work, so I don't really have enough free time for social interaction, even if I wanted it."

"Of course. Well then, I'll just brief you and be on my way. Mr. Hardy would like you to develop a new program to speed up the current blood screening process, to hire new analysts faster."

"I could do that, sure. But you're obviously aware that there will be an increase in risks associated with this? Speeding up the process will mean bypassing certain steps and procedures, therefore increasing risk."

"Yes, Mr. Hardy is aware of the risks associated by speeding up the process. But he insists that it be done. He accepts the risks."

The analyst hands Dr. Nichols some papers.

"Here are some operational parameters to work within, from Mr. Hardy himself."

Dr. Nichols scans over the papers for a moment.

"How soon is he expecting me to have something ready? I don't see a deadline date in here."

The analyst closes his briefcase and stands up.

"Mr. Hardy is expecting you to give him a brief on your screening program idea by the end of business today. You will receive more detailed instructions from him in person, at the meeting.

Please be seated in the executive conference room by fifteen after five."

"Today?"

"Is that a problem, Dr. Nichols?"

"No. No problem, I'll get it done."

"Good day, Dr. Nichols."

The analyst exits the office and is escorted by the lab technician again. Dr. Nichols stands and watches him walk away. "Little prick," he mumbles to himself. Dr. Nichols waits for Hardy's assistant to completely exit the lab before returning to his chair. Then he unlocks his drawer and pulls out a cell phone. He emplaces a SIM card and begins dialing.

"It's Will...I think we just found a break...Well, I'm not sure but I'll know more by the end of the day...Yeah...Yeah...Okay, I should be able to make that flight...Okay, I'll see you later tonight."

Dr. Nichols takes out the SIM card and locks the phone back up. He leaves his office and walks into the laboratory. He grabs his clipboard and begins making his hourly round of checks in his lab. Dr. Nichols pauses before he begins, staring at the dozens of Phase Three lab employees. He watches for a moment. All of them are slowly working, non-stop, like a mini zombie factory. He makes his rounds and stops by some of the technicians as he passes them. Some he remembers having laughs with, before they were Phase Three. Now they are just doing routine tasks, no joking anymore. Now they are filling injection bottles, placing labels on bottles and packages, just mindlessly going through their daily job, mindlessly going through life.

Were we really that different before all this started? Dr. Nichols asks himself as he continues walking through the lab. After he completes his rounds, he grabs a few test kits from the lab and begins working on the new screening program in his office. He starts right away and keeps his eye on the time, knowing that it is critical to meet Mike Hardy's demands.

* * *

Dr. Nichols pulls out a chair at the empty conference room table and looks at his watch, ten after five. He looks at his watch again, after a few moments of silence in the large and empty room. Fifteen after five. Chris Trendell opens the door.

"I'm sorry, Dr. Nichols. Mr. Hardy would like to do the brief in his office instead of out here. Please follow me."

Across the corridor, Tasha sees the two exiting the conference room and walking toward Mike Hardy's surveillance department. She wonders why Dr. Nichols is going to Hardy's department alone, and not with the other doctors.

"Sir, Dr. Nichols is here."

"Thank you, Chris. Would you like anything to eat or drink, William?"

"No, I'm fine. Thank you, sir."

The analyst shows Dr. Nichols to his seat and then leaves Mr. Hardy's office. He stands immediately on the other side of the door, visible through the glass window.

"You don't have to call me sir when it's just us. Please, call me Mike. So, how have you been, William? I think the last time we talked about anything other than work was at the Christmas party last year, at my father's house. Help us all, it's almost time for that party again." He smiles a little at Dr. Nichols.

"I'm good sir...Mike, thanks for asking. I'm staying pretty busy these days. Really focused on Phase Three implementation and making sure everything goes smooth in the labs."

"That's what I love about you, Will, your loyalty, your dedication. You don't mind if I call you that do you, Will?"

Dr. Nichols shakes his head in acceptance of him using an abbreviated version of his first name. It was eating him up on the inside though. Robert was really the only one that called him that, and Robert was his friend, not Mike Hardy.

"You definitely live up to your family's long history and reputation within The Society."

"Thank you, sir...Mike."

"Okay. Let's hear what you have for me."

Dr. Nichols hands over a folder to Hardy and pulls out a laptop from his briefcase. He opens a picture file with a design of the new screening program.

"The concept is pretty simple here. Basically, what we will be able to detect immediately, with this new rapid scanner, is body temperature and the percentage of dying or dead, red blood cells. As you are probably familiar with, the average regeneration rate of red blood cells is about four months, but regeneration is more frequent after each phase of our TSOMBIE injections. We see an average regeneration increase of twenty-five percent after Phase One in subjects, and up to seventy percent faster in Phase Two subjects. This equates to red blood cell regeneration rates of roughly three months and one month, respectively. Depending on where every cell is at in their life cycle, it could take roughly double that time for all cells to complete regeneration, and to become permanent carriers of the virus. But, the regeneration rates stay consistent after that. So, a larger percentage of dead blood cells, matched with the average increase in body temperature, should be able to give us solid confirmation of TSOMBIE infection during our new screenings. Obviously, it's not one-hundred percent accurate, and the complete screening will still need to be done. But, I think this will meet your intent."

"Impressive. That's truly impressive, Will, especially with the tight deadline I gave you today. So, how fast exactly are we talking about actually getting results with this new, 'rapid scanner system,' as you call it?"

"Well, almost immediately, sir. I would say within a matter of minutes to within an hour, max. And this all depends on the level of risk you are willing to accept, as far as accuracy goes. The larger the amount of blood to be analyzed, the more accurate, but with accuracy comes time. It's about eighty-five percent accurate within just a minute, ninety-five percent within an hour."

"This is great work, really! So, let's plan on this. We'll do the ninety-five percent test for new analysts being hired, and the eighty-five percent test will be perfect for our mass population testing program, after Phase Three is complete. Now, how long do you need to get this amazing new screening program up and running?"

"I think a month or maybe a little longer. That should be enough time to get the lab and machines set up, and get the scanners engineered and manufactured."

"You have two weeks. I can't wait any longer. We have an increased demand for analyst operations and well…well I have confidence you can make it happen William. My whole team is here to give you all the support you need. I look forward to seeing this in action, and please, keep me updated regularly on the progress."

Mr. Hardy motions to his analyst. The analyst steps back inside the office, holding the door open for Dr. Nichols to exit.

"Understood. Two weeks. I will need to make some trips to our other labs, to pick up some additional equipment. But other than that, I should have what I need to make it work."

"Great. Take care, Dr. Nichols."

Mike Hardy and his analyst watch him exit the department, escorted by a security guard.

"Do you want us to put a surveillance team on him sir? We're stretched thin, so we would have to reassign one."

"No, that's not necessary. I don't have any concerns about Dr. Nichols, unless he doesn't meet this deadline. Just keep an eye on his travel schedule, and if anything unusual comes up then we will start tailing him."

"Yes, sir. Would you like to do the daily update now? I have some new updates on Ms. McNeil's activities."

"Let's do it over dinner, Chris. I'll meet you at the executive club, say in an hour? I want to give the old man an update of this good news."

The analyst leaves the room. Hardy takes a seat in his chair. He smiles to himself, thinking about how impressed his father will be, now that they have a solution to their mass population testing method. One of the same problems they have been talking about for the past few months. He's even happier because he is the one bringing his father the solution, before Tasha.

TWENTY

"I'm going to grab another water. You want one?" Julia asks, wiping her hands on her jeans.

"Yeah. I think the holes are deep enough now. Anyways, I need a breather before we finish this up."

Julia walks back from the edge of the wood line, back towards the cabin. Dave takes a seat in the grass, the warden on one side and Mr. Roark on the other. He dozes off for a minute and is startled by Julia tapping his shoulder, handing him a bottle of water.

"Thanks."

Julia takes a seat beside him and they both drink water for a few moments, in silence.

"Okay, let's get this over with." Julia breaks up the silence and moves behind the warden's arms, ready to lift him up.

"Wait," Dave says. "We should remove his clothes first, and burn them or something, just in case. We don't want to make it that easy for them to identify the body, if he is found."

"Good call. We don't need to do that for Mr. Roark though, right?"

"No. I've already got his wallet and watch. Just check his pockets to make sure I didn't miss anything."

Julia begins searching Mr. Roark, with gentle care, as she watches Dave harshly ripping the clothes off the warden. She pauses. She feels some loose paper, deep in his back pocket.

"You got something?"

Julia pulls out the folded paper and reads the writing to herself, 'To the daughter I never had, Love Tommy.'

"Umm…Yeah, looks like a letter. I'll check it out later."

Dave sees the emotion in Julia's face but chooses not to say anything. He just continues removing the warden's clothes, fast and unemotional. Julia wants to read the letter in private, not there, not then. She regains focus on the task at hand and puts the letter in her pocket for later. She looks at Dave and they both continue working.

The sun begins to go down over the trees as they both stand in silence, over the now, freshly covered mounds.

Silence. No words of remembrance. No prayers.

They both knew that he was at peace and was a good man, and there was nothing that had to be said.

* * *

Julia grabs the bottle of whiskey as she heads to the bedroom and closes the door. She opens the letter and begins reading.

Dave and Amy begin packing. They also start searching the cabin for supplies they can use for the road, while simultaneously sanitizing any evidence of them being there.

A few moments go by and Julia wipes her cheeks. She uses her shirt to dry her eyes as she gets to end of the letter from Mr. Roark.

- P.S. Take nothing in this new world at face value, nothing. Apply your training to everything you see, everything. And most of all, Never Quit -

The sadness starts to go away for a moment and she lets out a small but comforting laugh, remembering Mr. Roark's comedic facial expressions and his awkward body language when he talked. She puts the letter back in her pocket and begins packing and searching, alongside Dave.

"Where's Amy?"

"She's taking a break. She's got to feed the baby, so she'll be ready to sleep once we start moving."

"Hey, I was looking for that earlier." Dave takes the bottle from Julia's hand and takes a sip.

They both take a few drinks and then continue searching the cabin. Julia starts a fire and starts bringing all the items needing to be burned over to the fireplace. They take a seat, watching the warden's clothes and Mr. Roark's bloody towels burn, together.

"Never Quit." Julia mumbles to herself as she takes another sip from the bottle.

"What was that?"

"Oh, sorry. Nothing. Just something Mr. Roark said in his letter."

"So I was thinking, we head east to Knoxville first. I know some people we can trust there, members of our old team. Maybe they're in contact with your dad or have an idea of where he is. What?" He asks, at Julia shaking her head.

"Well, we know that Mr. Roark knew where my dad is at. So, don't you think he would have written it down somewhere? I just can't believe he wouldn't write it down, as a backup, in case he...You searched his wallet, right?"

"Oh yeah, I tore that thing apart. Nothing useful in it, other than cash we're going to need for the road. I found some more cash hidden in the kitchen too. I looked every place I could think of in here, but I never found anything with an address or map, other than the one of this area. But he secmed in such good shape last night. I should have still made him tell me though, just in case, but I didn't..."

"It's not your fault Dave, or mine, or his. If he would have known he was going to die last night, he would have told us. No doubt. But he still would have had a backup plan. I know he had one."

Julia freezes with the bottle in her hand, passed halfway in the air to Dave. She stares at him, with large, surprised eyes.

"What?"

Julia quickly gives him the bottle and frantically pulls Mr. Roark's letter out of her pocket. She starts scrolling over the letter again, this time with excitement, not sadness.

"Quick, get me something to write with."

Dave returns from the kitchen with the briefcase and hands her a pen. Julia starts counting letters and circling some of them. She folds the letter in half and starts writing down all of the circled letters. Dave doubts what she is doing at first but then he starts seeing some real words appearing in Julia's writing, out of the inked up, circled letters.

"Wow, that's incredible. How did you know to do that? And how did you learn to do, whatever that was? Your dad?"

"I figured he would be too paranoid to keep the address in plain sight anywhere. At the end of the letter he said not to take anything at face value and apply everything I know. So I figured it was worth a shot, since that was the only thing we had with writing on it from him. It's just an old cipher decoding technique my dad taught me a long time ago. And look, it's in Nashville. I mean that's only about two hours from here. And that means we won't have to carry a lot of extra supplies and rations with us. We could be there by nine, tonight, if we leave soon. So, what do you want to do?"

"Well, traveling at night is a little more dangerous. But, we don't really know how long we will be safe here either. We don't know for sure if they will come looking for the warden anytime soon, or at all. Yeah, I think we should go tonight. But we need to get rid of his truck before we go. And I think I have an idea that will keep anyone from looking in the woods for his body, for a while anyway."

Amy comes out of the bedroom and quietly closes the door. She comes up and hugs Dave tightly, and gently kisses him on the shoulder.

"Samantha is fed and sound asleep, and I'm all packed and ready. What's all the commotion about? What are you guys talking about?"

Julia looks at Dave and he gives her the look back with his eyes that he will explain their plan to his wife.

"Finish packing, Julia. We will be waiting for you."

Dave walks with his wife to the kitchen and begins telling her the plan.

* * *

Julia finishes packing her backpack with the essentials, and then the briefcase. She walks into the living room after she's done and sees Amy and the baby, staged and ready to go by the door. Amy turns from the window.

"Well, I'm ready. So I guess we're really going to do this now. Where's Dave?"

Amy turns from the window and hugs Julia. Julia is shocked, but she feels relieved by her embrace.

"Thank you, Julia. I'm sorry I've been so, well, so short tempered. I know it's a good thing we left our house now, even though I didn't want to admit it at first. We wouldn't have been able to stay there forever, not without eventually needing help. I did want to stay here in the cabin a little longer though, you know, until our daughter grew up a little bit. Sorry, didn't mean to get all emotional on you." Amy wipes her eyelids.

"No, no, it's okay. And you don't have to be sorry. I can't imagine how hard it must be on you, on both of you. And I'm sure I seemed a little demanding when we first met. Showing up out of nowhere like that, without any notice, asking you to leave and go somewhere different."

"Thank you, Julia. Oh, right, Dave. He is just doing a quick sweep outside to make sure it's safe for us to move. He'll be back in a minute."

"Okay. I'm going to grab some extra bottles of water, just in case."

Julia walks over to the kitchen cabinets and puts a few more plastic bottles in her backpack.

"Are you an only child? Don't take this the wrong way or anything, it just seems like you're the type of daughter that their father raised like a son, because they never had one."

"Well…technically no, I'm not an only child. I have a younger brother. It wasn't that my dad tried to raise me like a son, he just didn't know how to raise a kid at all really, me or my brother. My mom was always home while my dad was away most of the time, in the military. But she was never really there, I mean, she didn't raise us. She was an alcoholic. I raised myself, and my brother for that matter, with a little help from my dad and his friends every now and then. Then my mom ran off and divorced my dad, taking my brother with her. She died shortly after that, and my brother stayed with his step-father. He wasn't a bad guy. And Brian had way more chances to live a better life there than he ever would have here, with me and my dad. It's been a while since I've seen my brother. I don't even know if he's okay from this, well whatever this is."

"Sorry, I didn't mean to…well, I think I'll just be quiet now."

"Oh, no. I'm okay, really. I actually enjoy having a conversation with another female for once."

Amy smiles and readjusts the baby in her arms.

"Well then, was there ever a 'special man' among all the men in your life? You are really beautiful you know."

Amy smiles and Julia smiles back, thanking her for the compliment.

"I had my eyes on a couple of guys I went to school with. I think I came off too boyish, too tough, for the ones I liked though. The guys I liked were always into 'normal girls.' I mean, they always invited me to go hunting with them, but nothing more, nothing romantic or serious. That, coupled with my dad coming off as a crazy war veteran, just scared off most guys considering me as girlfriend material. I've been on some dates before, and, well you know, I'm not a virgin or anything. I've never been in love though, or dated anyone I really liked before."

"Believe me, you're not missing much with the whole love thing, other than more stress. It has its moments, don't get me wrong, but life was so much easier when I was single."

Julia smiles but knows that Amy is just trying to make her feel better, and she doesn't care if Amy is telling the truth or not. She would give anything to go back a few years and really try to start a relationship, to start a family of her own. But she knows her chance for that had come and gone now, and there is no need to waste time or energy dwelling on it. Julia squints at a flicker of movement near the trail.

"Dave's back. I'm going to make one last sweep through the cabin and then I'll be out."

Julia starts combing the cabin with a flashlight, looking for anything they might need, or might need to still get rid of. Amy moves outside on the porch with the bags and baby.

"We're clear to leave. You ready? How's Samantha?"

"She's fine, still sleeping. Julia just went to check the cabin one last time and then she'll be out."

Julia turns at the backdoor before she leaves the cabin, stares briefly at the chair that Mr. Roark used to rock away in, at the couch he slept on, and then she closes the door.

* * *

They all make their way up the trail, uncover the SUV and get inside. Dave briefs them his plan of dumping the warden's truck into the nearby river. After of few minutes of debate and questions about the plan, they start moving out of the woods. They follow Dave to the river and he dumps the truck, as planned. Dave gets back in with them and they begin to drive down the long and dark highway, on their way to Nashville.

AMERICAN Z

TWENTY-ONE

Captain Brown walks to the bathroom and sticks his head down the stairs.

"Hey, Dr. Singer! I mean, Robert! I think your friend just pulled up! There's a car at the gate!"

Robert sees the car on the camera monitor. He sees that it's Dr. Nichols and he gets up from his chair and heads up the stairs.

"Thanks. He has the code to get in."

Justin walks back to the living room and sees the gate opening with the car coming through, to the back of the house. Robert pours a couple of drinks and takes a seat across from Justin in the living room.

"Thanks."

Justin takes one of the drinks that Robert sat down in front of him. Dr. Nichols walks in the living room and he and Robert shake hands, and then exchange a few light words. Justin gets up to introduce himself.

"Hi, my name is…"

"Captain Justin Brown, soon to be medically retired from the military, and then, Justin Brown. Married. No kids. Yeah, it's nice to finally meet you."

"Umm…yeah, okay. Nice to meet you too."

Justin looks at this man who seems to know everything about him.

He was similar in height and had a muscular build like Robert, but he had less hair and tones of gray showing. Clean shaven though, no neatly trimmed beard. Glasses. Nice suit. All very professional and doctor-like. Then he looks down and notices the ring on Dr. Nichols finger. He remembered seeing the same design on the pictures of The Society, in Robert's basement.

"Don't be alarmed kid. I'm one of the good guys. I'm going to help make you one of the good guys too. You're going to be our secret weapon to help us finally take down The Society, and to save our nation, to save the world!"

"Alright, alright, Will. Enough with the motivational speeches. What's the update?"

Robert lights up a cigarette and motions for them to follow him. They enter the basement and huddle around the big dry erase board, with notes written all over it. Dr. Nichols grabs a marker and starts writing notes and sketches for a few moments. Robert and Justin sit patiently, waiting for him to finish.

"Okay. So we know that The Society is looking to hire a mass amount of new analysts. We're still trying to confirm what exactly for, but I think it's to monitor their own kind, other members of The Society. They have increased security at the headquarters for one, and I overheard some other members talking about being followed home and around town. So, with the hiring of new analysts, the door is open for us to get you Captain Brown, in as an analyst, instead of a corporate pilot. And, this allows Julia to help out in other needed operations."

"Wait...Julia?" Justin interrupts, confused. Robert never briefed him on her part in all of this.

Robert motions for Dr. Nichols to continue.

"Hardy, the junior type, wants me to speed up the blood screening process for hiring new employees. Instead of waiting three weeks for results, I have to create a program to get them much faster. I'm talking from weeks down to hours, even minutes. This means that new analysts will be able to start work the first day they come in. And this means we can get Captain, we can get Justin, inside much quicker, to infiltrate their surveillance department. We really need to get you in the network department, but they're not hiring, the surveillance section is. The main thing is to get you in there quick, with this new opportunity. And, they won't have a reason to follow Justin for three weeks now, like they do with new employees, watching his every move while waiting on his blood results to come back."

Robert looks back at Dr. Nichols, from the notes and sketches he's been staring at on the board.

"So this is the new, big break? How are you going to be able to manipulate Justin's blood test that quick? I mean, this new scanner looks handheld. This could take total control over blood tests out of your hands. And we've fought too hard to get you where you are right now in the lab, in control of the testing."

"We talked about is Robert, them trying to get scanners designed for Phase Three implementation, so the virus can be detected in people almost immediately. That day was going to come regardless of whether or not I helped. At least if I, if we, design it first, then we'll know how it works and how to circumvent it."

Robert and Dr. Nichols look at each other and Robert seems to calm down after what Dr. Nichols just said. Dr. Nichols walks over to his briefcase and pulls out a small, black box that has a keypad and small lights on it. He holds it out and then looks at Robert and Justin. He walks over to Justin and grabs his hand.

"Hey! What are you doing?" Justin jerks his hand back and Dr. Nichols holds on tight.

"Calm down kid. Relax. Now give me your index finger."

Justin looks at Dr. Nichols with doubt and then at Robert. He slowly extends his index finger. Dr. Nichols places Justin's finger inside a small hole on the side of the little device, and then presses a few buttons on the keypad.

"Ough." Justin pulls his finger out and looks at the fresh drops of blood slowly coming out. He wraps the bottom of his shirt around his finger and stares at the black box with a little angst on his face.

"It's just a little pin prick, come on Captain. You sure he's yours?" He says to Robert. "Okay, now just give it a minute. And this machine is simple okay, red means not infected, green is infected."

Dr. Nichols stares at the small screen on the device in hands, and after a couple of minutes a little red light glows on top of the device. Dr. Nichols then takes a small vile of blood out of a little case. He changes out a clear sheet of film in the bottom of the black box. Then he places a small drop of blood from the vile onto a new sheet of film and hits a few buttons on the device again.

"Alright. Now, just another minute here."

Robert lights up a cigarette and finishes off his drink. A minute or two goes by and this time a green light begins to glow at the top of the device. Justin doesn't know what it really means but is still somewhat impressed that the little machine does something.

"Well, so much for not helping The Society. You're giving them exactly what they need to find all of the immune and uninfected!"

Robert refills his glass and calms back down. He knows Dr. Nichols is right, and it is better that they know exactly how The Society will test people in the future.

"Okay. You built it, so how do we bypass it?"

"I can explain it, of course, but I think it's best that I show you."

Dr. Nichols changes out the sheet of film in the device again. This time he sticks his finger in it. Robert stares at him with curiosity. A minute goes by and again, a green light comes on.

"Wait…how…he said you were immune." Justin is now more confused and doesn't know what is going on.

"I am. I am immune"

Robert and Dr. Nichols just look at each other, and then Robert grins.

Robert and Dr. Nichols had talked before about different theories of immune blood and virus interactions, and Robert knew what he had done.

"He injected himself with the virus, Justin."

"I don't understand. He's immune though, right? So how...?"

"We've known for a while that the immune can receive multiple doses of the TSOMBIE virus without turning, without ever becoming infected. But, we have never really analyzed ourselves, thoroughly that is, after testing it on us. I mean we never tested for simple things like temporary increases of blood temperature, which is exactly what happens when someone receives the virus, immune or not. The virus causes an increase in blood temperature. It was so simple, and it was right in front of us the whole time. I discovered by accident really. One night while running Phase Three tests on myself, exhausted by extremely detailed cell analysis, I gave myself a plain and simple, old-fashioned, physical exam. And well, the results of body temperature changes were pretty interesting. Phase One increased temperature almost a full degree Fahrenheit and lasted about twelve hours. Phase Two, a little over one degree and lasted a full day. And Phase Three increased my temperature by almost two degrees and lasted about thirty-six hours. So, I've designed these new screening devices to primarily test for blood temperature, that's what the light is synced to anyway."

Justin now understands how the little device works, and he thinks it is pointless.

"You don't have to be doctor to test someone's temperature, any store-bought thermometer can do that. And you don't need to draw someone's blood for that. Why the need for the pin prick? It looks to me like you just created a really fancy thermometer there, doctor. The Society is not dumb, according to both of you, so they have to know the full effects of the virus and they're going to laugh at your little device you built."

Dr. Nichols tilts his head to Justin's remarks. Justin sits back down and thinks to himself. He begins to think that he probably should have just kept his mouth shut.

"Are you done now?" Dr. Nichols looks at Justin and then continues talking.

"As I was saying, the primary function of the test that 'The Society' will think the device is for, is to analyze live and dead blood cell counts, not to primarily test blood temperature. Hence, the need for the pin prick, for a blood cell count."

Dr. Nichols pauses and looks at Justin. Justin sits a little deeper in the chair, now realizing he should have definitely kept his mouth shut.

"However, the numbers and data collected by the device will be too complicated for anyone to decipher right away. I mean other than myself, there are only a handful of doctors and scientists at AGI Headquarters that would be able to understand it. So this will keep me valuable to them and should keep me in control of the program, for a little while longer anyway. The first scanner I make for Hardy will need to be a little different than this though. I told him it would take hours to get results instead of minutes, to increase accuracy of results. But for the most part the device will be the same, I mean, all of the hard technology is here and done already. We have two weeks to work on camouflaging the defect in the design, which is the blood cell data does not trigger the light, just the temperature needs to do that. The Society will mass produce these based off my design, but production will be done by Phase Three employees. Those zombies don't have the self-conscious to discover the problem with the technology, they're just going to build the devices over and over again like, well you know, like zombies."

"Why didn't you ask me to help you with this, Will?"

"Come on, Robert. You have enough stuff to plan and work on already. I didn't want to ask for your help until I had something solid to work with."

"Well, it looks pretty good. Leave it here and I'll work on delaying the light sensor and put the finishing touches on hiding the defects."

Justin picks up the black box and studies it. Robert and Dr. Nichols toast their glasses and take a drink.

"I'm going to finish making us some dinner. Will, bring the young Captain up to speed on his future job, and who the members of The Society are at AGI Headquarters and how they are structured."

Dr. Nichols raises his glass to Robert as he heads up the stairs.

* * *

Dr. Nichols explains the hierarchy of The Society to Justin and how everything works at AGI. He also explains normal characteristics of Phase Three employees and how he will need to act once he gets inside, like a zombie. He answers Justin's questions and can tell Justin is anxious to begin training on how to infiltrate The Society. Their conversation gets interrupted when Justin sees a car pull up in the driveway, on one of the CCTV monitors.

"Is Robert expecting someone else tonight?"

He waves Dr. Nichols over to look at what he sees on the monitor. They watch a young woman get out of an older model SUV. She sits against the front fender facing the house, looking straight into the camera on the house that's aimed at her. Dr. Nichols stiffens up.

"Oh man. This is not good, not good at all. That's his daughter. That's Julia."

Dr. Nichols makes his way upstairs to tell Robert.

Justin sits back down and watches the monitor closely, trying to comprehend that he is about to meet his sister, his sister that he never knew existed until just recently.

Dr. Nichols enters the kitchen but it's empty. He sees steam coming from the stove but there's no sign of Robert. Then he notices that the front door is open.

Robert stops at the end of his sidewalk where Julia is now standing. They both lock eyes and stare at each other in silence.

Julia had worried that she would get emotional when she saw her dad again, if she ever saw him again. She had thought about this moment over and over again in her head for a long time. She had thought about what she would say, how she would react. But now that the moment was happening, she was too exhausted to react. Exhausted with anger, anger over the year in the bunker, and anger from what happened at the cabin. Emotionally drained from all that had happened, she couldn't really feel anything now. Now she just felt, numb.

Robert breaks eye contact first and looks in the SUV, at Dave and a young woman.

"Where's Tommy? Why didn't he call me?"

Julia looks up at the sky and takes a deep breath. And then she locks eyes again with her dad, but her eyes are filled with emptiness.

Robert knew what happened to Mr. Roark, without Julia having to say anything. He knew that Mr. Roark was gone as soon as looked at the cold darkness in Julia's eyes.

A light comes on in another house across the street and breaks his attention.

"You might have just compromised everything we've done, all the sacrifices we have made, by just showing up like this, Julia. Do you realize that?"

"Yeah, I'm fine, thanks for asking dad. Good to see you too."

She moves away from the fender and moves directly in front of him, their bodies almost touching now. She looks up at him.

"Believe me, if I had any place else to go, any place at all, then I would not be here. I had no choice but to come here. Now, you are going to let us stay here for as long as we have to, until we have somewhere else to go. And I'm not asking you this. Do you, realize that?"

Robert is about to say something, but he sees headlights from another car, from up the street in the neighborhood.

"We can't discuss this out here. Quick, just move the car to the back of the house. We can talk about it inside. I'll open the gate."

Julia rolls her eyes and gets back in the SUV.

Justin sees the car coming in the gate and he heads upstairs. He runs into Robert, standing with a weird look on his face near the door.

"Justin, pack up your stuff, and head on home for the night. Dr. Nichols will give you a ride back to your car."

"Is everything alright?"

"Yeah. Yeah, I think we're okay. Looks like our plans have definitely changed a little though. Anyways, I'm going to have my hands full tonight. Julia doesn't know about my other life yet. She doesn't know that you're my son either, her brother. And tonight is definitely not the night for her to find that out, on top of everything else."

"Sure. I understand. It's getting to be about that time anyway."

Justin starts packing his bag and then stops for a second. He looks at Robert and almost feels sorry for him, standing there in his own world of thoughts, alone.

"But for someone with personal experience in this area, the longer you keep it from her, the more pissed off she's going to be."

"I doubt it's possible to piss her off any more than she is right now. I'll call you when it's clear to come back over and continue training."

Justin grabs his bag and heads out the back door. He looks back as Robert and Dr. Nichols exchange a few words.

Then Julia and Justin pass each other on the stairs, without saying anything. They make eye contact for a brief second and then keep walking in opposite directions.

Justin gets in the car and sits quietly. He watches out the window as a man and another woman get out of the SUV, carrying a baby.

Dr. Nichols passes the group on the stairs a moment later as he walks to his car.

"Who was that with Robert's daughter?"

"I'm pretty sure the guy used to be in Robert's team, back in the military. I can't remember his name, but I've seen him a couple of times before, overseas. Not sure about the other girl and the baby. Maybe his wife? She looks kind of young for him though. Let's get out of here, before Robert or Julia blow the house up."

* * *

Robert continues cooking, keeping his back turned as the group comes inside. He hears the sound of a small child and the low, whispering voice of a young woman. He pauses for a second with disbelief about a child being in his house. Then he continues cooking without turning around.

"Dinner will be ready in a few minutes. I'm sure you all are hungry. The bedrooms are upstairs. You can go and get situated and cleaned up while I finish cooking."

Dave wants to say something, but he senses the frustration in Robert's voice and decides to keep quiet, until he calms down.

"Julia. I would like to talk with you for a moment please, alone." He still has his back turned to them.

Julia looks at Dave and Amy as they leave and walk upstairs. Robert waits until he hears the door close upstairs, and then he turns off the stove and turns around. Julia is exploring the living room. Robert follows her. She immediately notices one of the photos of her dad, and another woman she doesn't recognize. She knows it was taken a long time ago by how young he looks in the picture, and happy.

"I'm assuming you contacted Dave on behalf of Tommy, to try and help him. And I'm assuming that young woman is Dave's wife, and that is their child."

Julia turns and looks at him and then continues walking around the house, trying to avoid talking to him. Robert knows what she is doing and he knows she is probably analyzing the scenarios in her head about the house, about the photo, and what it all means.

"Look Julia, this is not the way I planned it but I'm glad that you are here now. And I'm glad you are okay. I'll give you your space and some time to decompress, but now that you're here, we do have a lot of things to start working on. And even though I feel for Dave and his, his situation, this can't be a permanent thing. I'll help them here in the meantime, but they can't stay here forever Julia. It's just too dangerous, not just for me, but for them too."

Julia wants to say something, anything to start an argument, but she can't. She knows that he is right. She knows that whatever her dad is planning and what he is involved in is dangerous, and it's no place for a mother and a child.

Robert walks back to the kitchen and sees Dave, now standing at the bottom of the stairs. Robert hesitates for a second and then begins fixing the plates. He wonders how much Dave overheard.

"He went peacefully, Robert. I thought you should know that. I did what I could, but, he was just too sick."

Robert stops what he's doing and turns slightly. He looks at Dave, thanking him silently for the comment.

"I didn't plan on this, Robert. The wife, the baby, seeing Tommy, coming here, none of it. I'm sorry I never reached out like you wanted me to, after this all started. When I found out Amy was pregnant, I knew it was my responsibility, mine alone, to protect her and the baby. I didn't think I would be any use to you then. But, we're here now, so whatever you need us to do then we'll do it. And if that's nothing and you just want us to leave, then I understand that too. Just give me a day or two, for Amy and the baby to rest, and to find some place safe. Then we will leave."

"More people to help is never a bad thing, Dave. I'm glad you guys made it this far, and I'm glad you got Julia back to me, safe. You can brief me tomorrow on the details of what happened at the cabin. Relax and get some rest tonight. And we can take some time to think about when you guys need to leave, and where you should go from here. I've got some work to finish up downstairs. I'll see you tomorrow."

Robert pulls a case out of one of the cabinets and opens it in front of Dave. Dave looks at the needles and small bottles in the case.

"I have to run some tests, to be on the safe side. You guys are not immune Dave, you know that."

Robert closes the case and hands it to Dave, making it his responsibility to draw the blood.

"Put them in the storage unit at the back of the refrigerator when you're done."

Dave understands that it has to be done and is not offended. And he knows what will have to happen if they are infected. Julia overhears them. She watches her dad go down the hall, into the bathroom, and closes the door.

* * *

Robert takes a seat in the basement and pours himself a drink while taking out a cigarette. He exhales deeply as he turns off the power to the internet and phone lines in the house. He lies down on the couch and tries to clear his mind, but it's racing nonstop. He keeps thinking of Julia.

He needed to do something to keep his mind off her, from getting emotional. He wanted to tell her he was sorry earlier, and that he loved her, but he couldn't.

He shifts to war-gaming all of the new possible scenarios of what would happen now, now that the plans have changed. He sits up and begins writing down notes and new plans. He knows sleeping is out of the question until he is able to empty out his frustration and anxiety.

Dave and Amy eat dinner in mostly silence, exhausted from the recent events over the past few days. Then they go to bed, relieved and feeling safe.

Julia pours herself a couple of drinks after dinner, attempting to help herself sleep and calm down.

She was definitely still angry at her dad, but she felt safe being there.

She drinks alone, in the quiet, mostly empty bedroom. Her exhaustion, mixed with the drinks, catches up to her and she falls into a deep and peaceful sleep, the first one in a long time.

* * *

The next morning Robert lays out the ground rules for the house and then goes to work. He takes the blood samples from Dave and his family to his office, and runs the tests. They all come back negative, not infected. After coming home and telling the good news to the new crew at the house, he briefs them all on the overview of The Society.

And he explains the current plans and operations he has been working on, on trying to prevent Phase Three. He answers their questions and explains everything to them in great detail, as he did with Justin.

Robert goes to work as normal each day, after explaining everything to them, and each day he gives them updates and answers more of their questions. Casual conversation, on the other hand, is almost non-existent from Robert. Amy doesn't really get involved in their discussions and normally just tends to the baby. Dave and Julia listen carefully to Robert's information and plans. Julia never speaks to Robert directly or asks him any questions. Robert knows she is doing it out of spite, but he keeps his word, and does not push her to get involved. Justin comes over every day and stays in the basement pretty much the whole time, training with Robert on his upcoming mission at AGI Headquarters. Justin tries to talk to Julia a few times, only to get one or two-word responses, or nonverbal expressions. The routines and attitudes of the house continue over the following days, and the days turn to weeks.

TWENTY-TWO

"This is truly great work, Dr. Nichols. At first, I wasn't sure if you would be able to meet the two-week suspense, but this is great." Mike Hardy says with enthusiasm, and with a devilish grin.

"Chris, update the current list of potential new analysts and start bringing them in on Monday for new screenings. I want our analyst staff to be increased at least twenty-five percent by the next executive meeting. And Chris, focus more on prior military or law enforcement when updating the new candidate list. This will reduce the field training necessary and help boost our numbers up even faster."

The analyst shakes his head and leaves the office. Hardy smiles at Dr. Nichols and takes a seat behind his desk.

"We're having a family get together at my father's house this weekend, Will. The old man was very pleased when I briefed him about this a few weeks ago, and I know he would personally like to thank you for your efforts. That is, if you are available of course, no pressure or anything?"

"Umm, yes, I can make it. Anything for you and your father, of course."

They shake hands and Dr. Nichols leaves the office a little happier. He sees this as another opportunity to strengthen his relationship with the Hardy's, and other Society leaders. And maybe, it could somehow help him gain access to the main server and finally get his hands on the restricted TSOMBIE files.

* * *

"Robert, it's me, Will. I've got some good news and bad news. Justin's definitely going to get added to the list of potential analysts. The only problem is that he might get assigned as a field agent based on his military background. You just need to fabricate something in his file to make sure he is more valuable to them behind a desk."

"Got it. That's too easy. The medical discharge that I gave him limits his physical capabilities anyways. I'll go back and add some more records to his military file though, computer technology training certificates, things like that. What's our timeframe here?"

"Well, they are bringing in candidates that have been on the waiting list starting next Monday. I guess I would say, make sure he is ready to go anytime within the next thirty days. I'll call you back at the normal time to talk about some other things."

Robert hangs up the phone and looks at Justin, studying over the board and his notes.

"What is it?"

"We need to double up on your training. We need to get you ready to go this month."

"Do you think that's enough time?"

"It has to be, this is our biggest window of opportunity. But if we don't do our best to make sure you're ready and you fail to remain undetected in there, then that's it."

* * *

Robert and Dave train Justin harder and longer over the next couple of days, and they are both pretty impressed by how well he does and how much he improves every day. They are confident in him and they are confident in their plans against The Society.

* * *

"Alright, I'm going upstairs to grab us some lunch. And Dave, go over the backdoor password methods again until he can get all of them right, on his first try."

Robert sees Julia sitting by the window in the living room, as he comes up from the basement and enters the kitchen. She's holding a picture in one hand and a small drink in the other. There's a freshly opened bottle of liquor on the table.

"So…is this why mom left you? She find out about this, other woman, here in the picture?"

Robert goes over and takes a seat across from Julia in the living room.

"She's pretty at least. Are we ever going to meet this mystery woman? Or did she run off and leave you too?"

Julia puts the picture down. Robert leans over and picks it up slowly. He looks at it for a moment.

"She's dead."

"Bummer." Julia says emotionless and takes another drink from her glass.

"Yeah. Well, she died a long time ago."

A moment goes by and neither one of them say anything.

"I want to talk to Brian. I want to let him know I'm alive. I want to know he's okay."

"We can't make contact right now, Julia. For now, everyone still needs to believe we are both dead. There's no chance at stopping Phase Three if we get caught. If you really care about Brian, then you will help me stop The Society. That's the only way anyone has a chance to be safe, immune or not."

Julia finishes her drink and puts down the glass.

"Okay, Dad, I'll do whatever it is you have planned for me. On one condition only. When I'm done, I get to see Brian."

Robert is about to say something, but Julia holds up her hand to stop him.

"And, part of that condition is you let me talk to him before I see him. After I do this training and before I go out there and start doing missions, or whatever it is you're calling it. I just want to hear his voice. That's my offer, no exceptions, take it or leave it."

Robert sits back in the chair quietly, thinking for a moment.

"Okay, Julia. Deal. I need to…"

"Robert! Robert!" Justin screams as he barges in the room and interrupts them.

"Sorry. Robert, can I talk to you a second? I need to show you something."

Robert wants to continue talking with Julia. He wants to tell her the truth about some of the things he is still keeping from her. He takes the interruption as a sign that it isn't the right time. He gets up and looks at Julia, then leaves with Justin out of the room.

"What? What are you so worked up about?"

Justin shows Robert an email on his phone, requesting that he come in the following week, 20 February 2019, for an interview at AGI.

"This is it Justin, this is it. Click accept at the bottom right there."

Justin clicks accept at the bottom of the email, and an attachment opens up with a welcome letter and an e-ticket for his flight.

"Alright. I'll go get Dave. We still have a few more days, so we need to make the most of them and keep training you. Don't worry Justin. Keep doing what you've been doing, you're almost ready anyway. And Will is always going to be close by, to help you if there are any issues at AGI."

Julia walks over to Justin with the bottle, after Robert leaves the room. She sits the alcohol down beside him without having to say anything. Justin looks at her in appreciation for the gesture and they both have a drink, in silence.

TWENTY-THREE

Justin looks over at the alarm clock. Almost five. It was set to go off in three minutes. He turns it off in frustration and looks over at his wife, still sleeping. He thinks about the long day ahead of him, and all of the unknowns it holds with it. He gets ready quietly, not to wake Claire, and then heads to the airport for his morning flight.

A few hours later and the shutter of the plane landing awakens Justin from his sleep, the sleep he didn't get from the night before. As soon as he gets off the plane he notices a couple of men in suits, standing in the lobby area with earpieces in. He avoids eye contact with anyone and heads straight for a taxi and to the address on the welcome letter.

The first impressions of AGI Headquarters appear to be like any other top business building in America. Nothing on the outside appears to seem weird or different. Justin observes the two men from the airport now walking toward his taxi. The effects of the shot he injected himself with that morning had already kicked in, and he begins to feel his muscle movements and reaction speed slow down. He thinks about having to inject himself every day, in order to appear like a Phase Three employee, to appear like a zombie. It makes him nauseous thinking about sticking himself with needles every day. He snaps out of it and regains his focus.

Justin sees more people watching him after he enters the main entrance. He remembers to stay calm and he doesn't panic or stare back. Then he gets funneled into a security checkpoint, along with several others after entering the building. Once on the inside of the building, Justin definitely realizes that this place is different. There are security personnel and cameras everywhere, not blatantly obvious to the untrained eye, but they are there. Justin waits his turn and goes through a fingerprint and retina scanner, and then is directed to another line with another security checkpoint. There is a large electronic device on a table at this checkpoint. Justin watches the person in front of him insert their finger into the machine and a few moments later, a green light comes on. Justin knows the machine, he knows what the machine is for, and is confident when he steps up.

Justin gets a green light.

A security guard looks at him and then at a tablet in his hands.

"Mr. Brown, proceed down the hall to interview room three."

Justin acknowledges calmly, and begins walking down the hall, slowly like he is sleepwalking. He can see the multitude of CCTV security cameras out of his peripheral vision, all along the hallway. The door opens automatically as he steps in front of the interview room. Justin goes in and sits at the table.

Up to this point, everything Robert told him about what would happen inside the building has been spot on. From this point forward though, in the interview room, is where the exact details were unknown. Justin sits patiently for several minutes, thinking about the harsh interrogation training Robert had put him through. He feels comfortable with the knowledge and skills he's been taught, and he remains calm.

The door opens.

An analyst comes in carrying a laptop. He sits down in front of Justin.

"Let's begin, Mr. Brown."

* * *

Julia and Robert both take a step back from the map board.

"That's it for the Midwest and West Coast contacts, and the key AGI facilities. Like I said before, those make up the majority of the non-infected to help us, and to help take out the facilities. And you understand the routes to use right?"

"Yeah. Got it." Julia says, unenthused.

"Alright. We're going to stick with that for now then. Most of your time is going to be spent out there anyway. We will tackle the East Coast last. There are fewer contacts, but it will be riskier out there, because most are near cities. And there's no need to take any unnecessary risks in the beginning. This way you will have time to perfect your tradecraft in a field environment. And you will have some experience under your belt before going to the more dangerous locations."

Most of what Robert was telling her was true, but the main reason he wanted to keep her away from the East Coast in the beginning was to not give her the opportunity to make contact with Brian. Not until he could be sure that she would keep her end of the deal first.

"Keep going over the routes with Dave today, until you have them memorized."

Dave shakes his head from behind a desk and Julia rolls her eyes.

"Everyone is packed and ready to go if anything goes wrong with Justin today, right?"

"We're ready." Dave replies.

Robert hands Dave a trigger mechanism.

"It has a one-hundred-meter range. And go straight to where we talked about if anything happens, no stops. I'll get there when I can."

Robert looks at Julia and then heads up the stairs. Dave follows behind him.

"When are we going to know something?" Dave asks, before he leaves.

Robert stops at the door, before leaving and going to work.

"Will is going to let me know when Justin leaves AGI and if there are any issues. We won't get confirmation that Justin has been hired until he makes it home, and it's safe for him to call me."

* * *

The day drags on slowly for Robert, watching the phone, waiting for the call from Dr. Nichols. Julia and Dave study the maps all day back at the house, constantly watching the phone, ready to leave at a moment's notice.

* * *

"Hey Julia, he's home. Finally. Let's go upstairs and find out what happened."

Dave hurries up the stairs. Julia stares at the map for a moment, looking at North Carolina, thinking about how Brian is doing. She takes a breath and puts him at the back of her mind. She doesn't want Brian to be a distraction for her. She wants him to be the motivation for her to stay alive, and for her to help stop The Society, for both of them. She sits down and begins writing the directions and routes again, memorizing them.

"So? How did it go? Did he get in?" Dave asks impatiently.

"I'm still waiting on Justin's call to see how the interview went. Will confirmed there were no issues inside of AGI with the screening and that Justin made it back on the plane safely. Justin is only going to call after he gets home and makes sure that he wasn't bugged or followed."

Robert pours a drink for himself, and then one for Dave.

"How did the training go today?"

Dave takes a drink.

"It went good. Julia's amazing. She has a real knack for this stuff. There's no doubt that she's your daughter. I think she's going to do great out there."

"Good. I'm glad to hear it. I want to push her out on the road as soon as possible."

Julia walks into the kitchen and interrupts their conversation.

"So, did the great Captain Brown get in?" Julia asks sarcastically as she ignores Robert's offer of a drink.

"I'm still waiting on his call to confirm."

About an hour goes by and they all sit down to eat dinner, all in silence, all waiting for the call. They eat slowly, ready to leave quickly and either go into hiding, or celebrate a small step forward.

Robert's phone rings.

Everyone lowers their forks.

He answers.

"Yeah…Yeah…No, not yet…Okay, I will."

Robert hangs up the phone and shakes his head no. Another few moments of silence go by.

"What's the backup plan if he doesn't get hired? You never told all of us that part, just Dave."

Robert takes a drink and looks at Julia. He is about to respond to her comment and then his phone rings again.

"Yeah…Okay…No, you will be fine…Alright…No, I'll get the address from him later…You are going to be working with him direct from here on out…Okay…Good luck."

Robert hangs up the phone and takes a deep breath. He looks up at everyone staring at him, waiting for a response. He smiles and raises his glass a little in the air. Everyone smiles with relief and takes a drink, everyone but Julia. She goes back to eating, in silence.

"The Society is moving Justin and his wife near the AGI Headquarters this week. He will start working as a surveillance analyst next week. We probably won't see him again until this is all over. And based off Dave's assessment, Julia, you're almost done with your training. You're going to begin your missions by the end of this week."

Julia drops her fork in midair, on top of the plate, creating an awkward moment of tension.

"I guess we better get back to it then. Dave, shall we?"

Julia puts her dishes in the sink and heads back to the basement. Dave kisses his wife and looks at Robert, then quickly follows behind Julia. Amy smiles awkwardly at Robert and then they quietly continue eating their dinner.

TWENTY-FOUR

Justin tries to unwind after his stressful day. He explains the new job at AGI and the upcoming move to his wife. She seems happy about it, but it only lasts a little while and then she goes back to her normal, quasi-zombie personality. Justin looks at her and again he remembers all of the great times they had together when they first got married, before all of this.

He knew they would never have those moments again, regardless if they succeeded or not. But, he had to help stop Phase Three from happening. Even though she wasn't like she was before, Justin had accepted the way she was now, and he had become used to making the best of their situation.

* * *

A few days go by and after the movers finish loading the trucks, Justin and his wife start driving to their new home.

They get settled in late at night. They get settled in and Justin tries to adapt to their new life of being monitored all of the time. Dr. Nichols had informed Justin of the normal camera and microphone locations in AGI employee houses, like his. Within a few hours of careful observation, Justin had located all of the cameras and microphones, as well as the blind spots. There weren't many blind spots, but it still gave him a little peace of mind to know he could take a break from it all when he needed to. He knew he still had a fraction of privacy left.

* * *

And it began. Just like that, Justin was a Phase Three analyst of AGI. Just like that, Justin was now working inside of the most powerful organization in the world. Dr. Nichols had duplicates of Justin's phone, his social media pages, and his email accounts. It was so he could help Justin decipher any direct messages from The Society.

The first couple of days were rough for Justin. He was still adjusting to living a very strict and dull daily routine, almost down to the minute. When he arrived at work, how many times he used the restroom, how long he stayed in the restroom, what he ate for lunch. Everything was routine.

His job was pretty simple though, and low level, all things considered. He was assigned a group of targets, Society members, and then he monitored them on cameras. Every day, the same thing. He watched them, tapped in on their conversations, and then he typed everything they did or said into a report. Simple, repetitive, boring.

His job was also pretty lonely. He was surrounded by several other analysts but none of them talked to each other, not casually anyway. Justin knew that they were all infected with Phase Three, but to him they all just looked like normal employees. They appeared to be normal employees, employees that were just focused on their everyday work, and employees that had really boring personalities.

Every night he fed his updates to Dr. Nichols, so he could pass them on to Robert. Justin didn't know what any of the updates really meant, but this is what they wanted him to do. And he trusted them. And he trusted that what he was doing mattered.

TWENTY-FIVE

"Everything you need is in your new car, Julia." Robert says, pointing over at the luxury sedan beside them in the hospital parking lot.

"There is more than enough cash in the suitcases, and the guns are under the seats. The medical supplies are in trunk, along with the research papers that justifies your reason for travelling. All of your identifications will pass inspection. The only thing you really have to worry about is Society members, so steer clear of large crowds in city environments. And remember, they have the ability to access any networked security cameras.

"I've got it. We have been over this a thousand times already."

"Sorry. You're right."

Julia looks away and opens the door. Robert grabs her arm and she looks back at him.

"Be safe, okay, be safe."

She can actually see the concern in his face.

Robert lets go of her arm, not to show too much worry, or any real emotions.

Julia quickly shakes off his mild attempt at being a father and gets in the car beside them. She begins to drive away, and Robert watches the car fade slowly out of sight.

Julia drives toward her first stop on her route, Missouri. She drives, filled with nervousness about the unknown ahead of her.

But still, the thrill of it all excited her just the same. She felt more complete, now after her father had told her everything that had happened, and about The Society. She felt more complete, now that she had a sense of purpose in her life and wasn't cooped up in some hole in the ground, or cabin in the middle of nowhere. She knew that what she was doing mattered. She also knew that the faster she was done, the faster she could see Brian again.

* * *

Robert comes home.

He felt somewhat relieved that everything was finally falling into place, after years of planning and a couple of setbacks. For the first time, in a long time, he felt mildly happy and enthusiastic. His mood quickly changed as he pulls into the driveway and sees Dave, sitting on the back porch, waiting.

Robert walks up the steps slowly. He leans against the rail at the top and lights a cigarette. Dave is not ignorant, he thinks to himself. He knows now that Justin and Julia had finished their training, there is no need for me to keep the three of them around anymore.

"I already told Amy. We're packed, and she understands. She's not upset or anything. Besides, I think she kind of liked it better out there in the woods. No offense."

Robert cracks a smile.

"I still need to gather a few more items for you, before you leave. So, you guys can relax for a couple more days. Let's grab something to eat, we can talk about all that later."

They walk inside the house and Robert pats Dave gently on the shoulder.

He liked having Dave around the house now. He liked having all of them around the house now. But he buried that feeling deep within himself. He wouldn't let his feelings jeopardize everything. He knew that what he was doing mattered too much for that, it mattered too much for everyone.

* * *

Julia pulls over after driving most of her first day, and she makes a phone call.

"Yes...I saw your ad in the paper about a cleaner...Yes, I know it...The Sink Only Makes Bubbles In The Evenings...Okay..."

Julia quickly writes down a number. She hangs up the phone and dials the number she just wrote down.

"Yes...It's clean...No, he's fine...Me? I'm his daughter...Okay..." Julia writes down an address. "...I can find it...Yeah...Okay, I'll be there."

Julia hangs up the phone again and drives to the address. It is a small restaurant off a main highway exit. Her phone rings when she parks.

"Is that you in the black car that just pulled up?" A man's voice asks.

"Yes."

"Come inside and sit in the third booth on the left. Keep your phone on. Do you have earphones?"

"Yeah, I have some."

"Good. Put them in after you order, and we will continue talking."

Julia keeps her phone on and walks inside the restaurant. She sees the empty booth and slowly walks towards it, making mental notes about her surroundings and everyone in the restaurant. Nobody seems to notice her. Everyone is either looking at their phones or watching the television screens. The waitress comes over and takes Julia's order. Julia puts her earphones in, which is about the only luxury of the cheap phones they use.

"We won't stay here long. I had to make sure you weren't being followed."

"I understand. So, are, all of you here right now?" Julia says as she scans the restaurant, trying to identify them.

"Yes, all three of us are here. And don't look around like that. You'll draw attention to yourself. One brother is sitting here with me and my youngest brother is in the car. We are the only ones in Missouri that I'm aware of. Do you have any brothers or sisters? You look like you're around my age."

"Umm, yeah, I have a younger brother. I haven't seen him in a long time though. You guys are all...real brothers?"

"Yep, I wouldn't be here if it wasn't for them. I don't know how you are doing this by yourself, all alone out here. Your father must trust you a lot to do this."

"Yeah, I guess you could put it like that. So, how do you know my father? You couldn't have served with him in the military if you said you were my age."

"Our father served with him. He got killed overseas on a deployment, a while back. Your dad reached out to us after the funeral."

A young man walks by and taps her table as he passes. She watches him sit down in front of another young man at the other end of the restaurant.

"We're safe. You don't have anyone following you. Finish your food and then you'll follow us to our place. We can talk about things in detail and the plans once we get there."

Julia eats and watches the two young men, one probably in his late teens, and the other in his early to mid-twenties. She watches them and thinks about what it would be like to eat dinner with Brian.

She finishes eating and follows them back to their little manufactured home, deep in the woods of Missouri. She lays out the plans in great detail and answers their questions as they come up. She shows them how to take down the critical AGI facilities within their state and Illinois, since it was close enough for them to do it. And there were no other contacts in Illinois or other surrounding states. She gives them enough cash to get all of the supplies they will need to accomplish their missions and then some extra, just in case.

* * *

Julia stayed with the Missouri brothers for almost a week, until they had the plans memorized, just like her. She trained them on small arms weapons, self-defense, and most importantly, how to make bombs. She enjoyed her time with them. Two of the brothers were close to her age and the younger one reminded her of Brian. But she knew that eventually she had to leave. This was only her first stop and she still had a lot of miles to go, and more contacts to meet, convince, and train.

* * *

So, she left. Julia continued on her mission, heading west and stopping in the states that had contacts in them. Most of the contacts were all the same, prior military team members of her father, or kids and family of his old team members. They all lived secluded, off the grid somewhere, patiently waiting to do their part and help save the country. Maybe even the world for that matter.

TWENTY-SIX

Several weeks go by, and then months. Robert is kept updated by both Julia and Dr. Nichols, on their progress. Julia's expedition was proving to be somewhat more productive than Justin's assignment within AGI. Julia's first mission from the Midwest and West Coast was coming to an end now and she would be heading back soon, back to Tennessee.

TWENTY-SEVEN

Robert asks Dr. Nichols to come down for a meeting on the night that Julia is scheduled to arrive back. He wanted to do a full debrief with both of them and change or update any of their plans, if necessary. He knew that if anything needed to be changed, then they needed to do it now, while there was still time.

Robert comes home from work and waits anxiously for both of them to arrive.

He would never admit it, but he had missed being around other people, ever since everyone left his home, months ago. He was fine before they all showed up to his house that night. It seemed like such a long time ago now. But after being exposed to human interaction for that short period of time, he was anxious to feel it again. It wasn't an overwhelming desire, and he still placed his mission first, but the feeling was still there nonetheless.

Julia arrives first, and Dr. Nichols arrives just a minute after. Robert greets Julia at the door.

"Welcome back. Great job out there."

"Yeah, thanks. I need a drink."

She sits her bag on the floor and walks right past Robert, into the kitchen.

"Yeah. Of course."

Robert leaves the door open for Dr. Nichols and follows Julia in.

"Dr. Nichols," Julia says to him while pouring herself a drink.

She stayed dry the whole time she was on her mission. It had been months since she had a drip of alcohol. She knew she wasn't an alcoholic, like her mom was, but definitely missed having a drink at the end of the day to relax.

"Julia, welcome back," he replies, seeing that she is not pouring him a drink.

There was always a sense of tension between him and Julia. He assumed it was because he was part of Robert's secret life, the one she never knew about it. And he didn't blame her for having those feelings, it was to be expected.

"Thanks, Doc. So, where's your boy wonder at?

"He won't be able to travel anytime soon. AGI is working their Phase Three analysts around the clock."

Robert pulls a fresh bottle of liquor from the cabinet and sits it down, seeing that Julia is not intent on sharing the one she has.

Julia notices what he's doing. So she deliberately pours herself another drink with her bottle, not needing a refill when she does it. She takes a long, slow sip, looking at both of them.

"I have dinner started on the grill for us. I thought you might like a nice home-cooked meal, after eating on the road for so long."

"Sure. Whatever. I'm going upstairs to unpack and take a shower."

Julia takes her glass and heads upstairs. She sees the door closed to Dave and Amy's room when she passes it.

She already assumed that they would be gone by the time she got back.

She knocks on the door anyways.

"Dave? You guys in there?"

Julia opens the door to an empty room, no bags or clothes anywhere, and the bed is made. Julia closes the door and takes a long, warm shower, and then returns downstairs. Dr. Nichols and Robert are eating at the table and a plate is made, waiting for her. She grabs her drink and sits down to eat. She starts eating, quietly, without looking up.

Robert can tell she is upset, upset that Dave, Amy and the baby are all gone. He starts up his conversation again with Dr. Nichols. They begin talking about accessing the main server at AGI.

Julia gently puts her fork down and picks up the phone next to her plate. A number is written beside it.

"What is this?"

"I'm keeping my part of the deal, a phone call to Brian after you made it back. That was part of the deal, wasn't it?"

"How do you know I haven't called him already? While I was out there by myself, alone, again."

"I know you didn't because you told me that you wouldn't. And I trust you, Julia."

Julia stares at her dad for a moment and then at the phone. She takes the phone and goes upstairs to her bedroom. She closes the door, locking it, and takes a seat on the bed.

She had contemplated calling Brian while she was on the road, traveling from state to state by herself. And it wasn't the deal with her dad that kept her from doing it, it was the fear of what she would say. Just like when she called him at the gas station near the cabin, and she didn't say anything.

Would he even recognize my voice? Would he believe me? Would he be angry at me? All of these thoughts begin rushing back through Julia's mind again as she stares at the phone in her hand.

* * *

Julia takes one last deep breath and dials. The phone rings a few times and then someone picks up.

"Hello?"

It sounds like Brian and Julia is quickly filled with excitement and emotions, all over again. She can't speak, again.

"Hello?"

Julia clears her throat. "Umm…Hello. Who am I speaking with?

"Brian. Who is this?" He asks calmly, with no infliction, monotone.

"Sorry, I must have the wrong number."

"Okay. Bye."

The phone goes dead.

"Goodbye." Julia says softly into the phone, only herself on the line.

She calms her emotions and laughs quietly to herself, while wiping her face.

She felt relieved just to hear his voice again, even though it was just for a brief moment. She wanted to share her excitement with Amy and Dave, the only ones she had really talked intimately with about her brother. But they were gone now.

Julia's brief moment of happiness subsides, and she becomes frustrated again, in the presence of reality.

She marches downstairs and returns to the table. Again, she eats without looking up or saying anything.

Robert ends his conversation and gives Dr. Nichols the signal that it's time to go downstairs. They get up and start walking down the hallway towards the basement. Robert stops at the bathroom door and looks back at Julia.

"Julia, please join us in the basement when you are done so we can start the debrief and go over the plans for the next few months."

Julia looks up at him and then continues eating, putting her head back down. She takes her time. She thinks about Brian and about finishing what she started with her dad, so she could be with him again. She finishes her dinner, and her thoughts, alone.

* * *

"Okay, let's get started," Robert says, walking toward the map board.

"Based on Julia's contact reports, the states that are highlighted in green are committed to helping. There are still a couple of contacts that are in limbo, and two that are completely out now. But, we may be able to work around that by splitting up one of the groups. The next priority for Julia is the East Coast contacts."

Robert points to the areas on the map that are circled and crosses out some of the contact names.

"The East Coast will be the most challenging. There are more AGI facilities and Society members, and there are fewer contacts to help, if Julia gets in trouble. So, the goal here will be to target the most vulnerable and high payoff facilities. But in order for this to work, we are going to need 'all' of the contacts to commit and be on board."

Robert highlights the key facilities on the map with his pointer.

"Julia, I want you to go back through the contacts you already talked to and see if any of them would consider going that far east to help, if it came down to that. Now, even though Justin's progress hasn't been as far reaching, we have still learned a few things of importance since he's been inside AGI. We now have confirmed that The Society is monitoring their members, as well as their family members. Even friends of Society members are being monitored. There are also more immunes out there than we know about, and we suspect the Inner Circle of The Society has a list of all of the bloodlines by now. We think that a copy of the list is on the main server, along with the secrets of how their messaging actually works on people, once they are infected."

He pauses for a moment and looks at Dr. Nichols.

"We have to find a way to access the main server, Will, and get those restricted files. We have to find out what is on them. We have to confirm if that is even where they are keeping their innermost secrets about the TSOMBIE program."

Robert pulls out a cigarette, still looking at Dr. Nichols, now waiting for him to brief his part.

"I have the backdoor program ready to go. I just need to get it on a computer that is connected to the main server lines, with someone who has the password on their computer. Hardy's computer is still the best option. I just have to find a way to get the virus on his computer. A thumb drive or disk. His little 'minion' is always in his office when I see him though, and he always takes my memory stick from me and puts it on his computer first. I just need to get a minute alone with Hardy's computer. I really need a diversion."

Dr. Nichols stops for a second and starts thinking about how to get on Hardy's computer. He snaps out of it and continues his brief.

"And speaking of Hardy, I have to give routine updates to him about the new rapid scanner machines I built. I have been stalling for as long as I can, but if I don't give them the finished product soon, then I basically risk losing my position. It will only be implemented at AGI and Society buildings at first, so it won't be a threat to Julia's mission. She should still keep some Phase Three doses to inject herself though, just in case."

"I agree. And keep trying to get on his computer. We only have a couple of months left before they start shipping out all of the Phase Three injections. Now, we need talk about the backup plan, should this whole thing go sideways, and we fail."

Julia and Dr. Nichols both sit up, now more attentive. Robert finishes his drink before he starts talking again.

"Dave is stockpiling supplies for our bunker, he has been doing that for a while now. We will have enough supplies for all of us to survive, for almost a decade, give or take. Hopefully it does not come to that, but we have to prepare for failure."

"Wait? What bunker? Not the same one you put me in?"

Robert looks at Julia. "Yes. Look Julia, I know how you must feel about that, but that bunker is the safest place for us."

Julia explodes from the chair, her face full of anger. But before she speaks, she closes her eyes, takes a deep breath and sits back down.

Robert knows he probably should have avoided saying that, but it's too late now. He waits patiently and quietly for her to calm down.

Dr. Nichols puts his head down to avoid any further tension in the room.

"Okay, so I am going to pretend, you didn't just say, what I think you said...that you know how I feel about that bunker!" She pauses and takes another breath.

"And what about the game warden? I know Dave told you about him. What if the cops know about it?"

"Dave has already investigated it and confirmed that we are in the clear. They wrote his death off as an accident. Nobody has been out there, and nobody is looking for him."

Julia gets up, infuriated again.

"I Am Not! Going Back! To That Bunker!"

Julia storms off, up the stairs and slams the bathroom door behind her. Something falls off the wall from the hard force of the door, vibrating and echoing through the house.

Robert lights a cigarette.

"Robert, I hate to think about it, but I need to ask you."

"You don't have to ask, Will. Of course, we will take care of him for you. Come on. Let's have a drink before you leave. It will be a while before we see each other again."

"Thanks, Robert. What about Julia though? Is she going to be okay? She seemed...pretty upset there."

"Yeah, she'll be fine. She is about as tough as they come. She still hasn't forgiven me for what I did. What can you do though? I still wouldn't go back and change what I did, to protect her."

They walk upstairs, and Robert places the towel hanger back on the wall, which Julia had knocked off.

"You think she will ever forgive you, Robert?"

"Maybe. Maybe not. But if we don't succeed then it really doesn't matter anyway, does it?"

* * *

The next morning Robert heads downstairs and starts the coffee pot. He pours himself a cup and walks into the living room. He turns on the television and sits down. He notices Julia's bag sitting next to the door.

Julia comes out of the bathroom and into the kitchen. She pours a cup of coffee and sits down on the opposite end of the sofa from Robert.

"You're up early. I figured you would want to sleep in and relax, after just getting back last night. You must be tired?"

Julia drinks her coffee and watches the news on the television, without responding.

"What's with the bag? You're not planning on leaving today, are you?"

Julia glares over at him.

"Is there some reason why I can't leave today?"

"No. I just thought…I mean it might be nice for just the two of us to spend some time together. There are still some things I need to tell you, things that you deserve to know. I know how you feel about me Julia, but I am still your father, and you are still my daughter. No matter how much you hate me for what I did, I did it to protect you, and I would do it again."

"What do you want from me?"

Robert sits down his coffee and slides over, closer to Julia, gently touching her arm.

"I want you to forgive me, Julia."

Julia pulls back, sliding away from him. He lets go of her arm at the rejection.

"Look, obviously whatever you still need to tell me is not going to help me complete my mission for you. Otherwise, you would have told me months ago, before I first went out there. So, evidently, it's not that important. Or it's just something else you lied to me about, that will upset me even more. Either way, I can't do this right now. I need to stay focused on finishing this and staying alive out there."

What she said made sense, and Robert respected her wishes.

"Well, it's your call then. If I don't see you tonight when I get home…be careful out there, Julia."

Robert and Julia look at each other for a second, and then he walks to the kitchen and refills his coffee. He doesn't look back. He walks to his bedroom to get ready for work.

Julia finishes her last bit of coffee and walks to the door, with the bag now at her feet. She looks back and thinks about going back to tell him how she felt.

Deep down she still loved him as her father, even after all he put her through.

She turns back around and picks up her bag, softly closing the door behind her as she walks to the car.

Robert hears the door close and then the car engine start. He goes into a daze as he stares at himself in the mirror. Everyone had left the house, again. He stares in the mirror, alone, again.

TWENTY-EIGHT

"Well, well, well. Look at what we have here. My, my, these Phase Three analysts are getting better looking by the week." A female voice says.

Justin feels a hand slide over his shoulder, and then a finger, gently down his back. He remains calm and remembers not to react quickly. He continues collecting his papers off the printer, pretending to ignore the new situation he suddenly found himself in.

"Stop. Turn around and let me get a good look at you."

Justin slowly turns around, maintains his composure, and looks straight at the beautiful woman that was talking to him, now standing face to face with her.

He knew right away who she was, remembering the pictures in Robert's basement. She was a key Society member, someone of importance. He also remembered seeing her with the other Society leaders around the headquarters building.

"What's your name handsome?"

"Justin. Justin Brown, ma'am."

"Ma'am? Good looking and a gentleman. Why does Michael get all of the good TSOMBIE analysts?"

Justin remains calm as the woman gently touches his chest.

"Tasha! Tasha!" Mike Hardy yells from his office while walking up to them.

"Do whatever you want with your Phase Three employees but leave mine alone. What are you doing over here in my department anyway?"

Hardy looks over at his right-hand assistant, upset he had not been informed that Tasha was there, in his surveillance department. He looks Justin up and down for a second.

"And you. Get back to work."

"Bye, Justin…" Tasha's voice fades, while being physically escorted out by Hardy.

Justin turns back around to the printer and continues retrieving his papers, slowly, and exhaling deeply.

"What are you doing over here, Tasha?"

"Your father wants to talk to us. Calm down, Michael. And he wants you to bring Dr. Nichols as well."

"Dr. Nichols? Why? Dr. Nichols works for me and reports to me."

"I don't know, Michael. I mean, you know how your father is. When someone does something good for The Society, you know, he likes to honor them, a lot. I think he wants to congratulate him in person again.

"He already did that though, at the party. And yes, I know how my father is about boasting accomplishments."

"Well, he's got some international Inner Circle members in his office, so…"

"Yeah, I got it, thanks."

Hardy is somewhat upset that he will not get all of the credit for the scanner accomplishment, but he is still satisfied that he is part of it, and not Tasha.

Justin collects the last page and returns to his desk. He watches the group exiting the department and looks down quickly as Tasha turns around at the door.

She looks toward his desk and then whispers something into another female's ear, and the other woman takes note of whatever Tasha says to her.

* * *

Justin finishes his shift and had almost forgot about the incident from earlier that day, until his, AGI issued, cell phone pings with a message. Justin reads the message before he starts driving home.

- Come to 372 Valley Oaks Drive at 9 p.m. You will receive further detailed instructions after you arrive. -

There is a bar code image on the screen as well, at the beginning of the message. Justin quickly pulls a disposable phone out his glove box. He calls Dr. Nichols on speakerphone as he begins to drive home, to avoid a delay in his routine driving time from work.

"Hello?"

"It's me, we have a problem."

"Give me a second." Dr. Nichols closes his door. "Okay, go ahead."

"Look at the message on my phone."

Dr. Nichols unlocks his drawer and opens the clone of Justin's, AGI issued, work phone. He reads the message. He immediately recognizes the address, and he knows what this is about.

"Okay, just calm down kid."

"Calm down? This is not a normal message! What is this about?"

"Everything is fine, we aren't busted or anything. Look, I can't talk right now, I'm still at work. I'll call you at the regular time tonight and explain."

Justin hangs up and finishes driving home, somewhat at ease but is still anxious to find out what the message means.

He arrives home. Avoiding his wife, glued to the television, he begins his normal routine of showering first. He stares at the phone in his hand, waiting for Dr. Nichols to call.

"It's about time. Alright, so tell me."

"So, the good news is we might have a way into the communications department."

"Okay? And the bad news?"

"Well, there's no easy way to put it kid."

"Just tell me then."

"The bad news is, you are going to...you have to cheat on your wife tonight."

Justin sits there for a moment, seriously confused about what he just heard. The comment came from way out of left field for Justin. That was never in the possibilities of all the scenarios he had been running through his head, while waiting for the call from Dr. Nichols. Then he stops, and thinks back to the incident that occurred earlier that day. And then he knew, he knew what Dr. Nichols was talking about.

"Are you, are you sure that is what this message means?"

"That is Tasha McNeil's address. All of the senior Society members from AGI Headquarters live in the same area. And it's no secret that Ms. McNeil likes to, well she likes to test out the product. And by product, I mean Phase Three employees." He pauses for a response. "You alright kid?"

"Umm, no. Not really. This never, never crossed my mind. In all of the things I thought I might have to do once I was inside, I never thought of this. And I know I don't have a choice, so please, spare me one of your motivational speeches right now."

There's a brief moment of silence on both ends of the line.

"Well then, any advice on how to handle myself, once I'm in her house?"

Another moment of silence goes by, but shorter.

"Just remember, you are supposed to be Phase Three. So, anything that she tells you to do, well, then you have to do it. Prepare yourself mentally for that and remember what you are doing all of this for. Remember, this is bigger than just you and your wife here too. Let me know when you make it back safe. But you are on your own once you're inside. Good luck kid."

Justin hangs up the phone and comes out of the bathroom. He sits down at the kitchen table and begins eating dinner with his wife, on schedule as normal.

"I've got to go back to the office tonight. I'll be back late." Justin says without looking up from the table.

"Okay. I'll make another plate for you, for later."

Justin smiles softly and quickly looks back down at the table, feeling shameful about what he is going to do later that night.

He completes his normal after-dinner routine and goes to bed, beside his wife, facing away from her.

* * *

Justin gets back in his car.

Ashamed. Embarrassed. Guilty.

He looks at his watch. After midnight.

He sends Dr. Nichols a text on his disposable phone, letting him know it was done. He starts driving back home and tries to clear his mind of what he just did.

He smokes a cigarette in his driveway when he gets back, staring at his bedroom window, where Claire was fast asleep.

She is innocent in all of this, he thinks to himself. Am I doing the right thing here?

He smokes another cigarette, delaying going inside.

He carries on a debate with himself for a few moments, until one side eventually convinces the other that he is doing the right thing. He convinces himself that he is doing what it takes to save her, to save himself, to save others. He commits to continue doing whatever it takes to save her. Lying, cheating, killing, he would do it. He would do it for her.

And even though he was fully convinced that he was doing the right thing, something changed in Justin that night. He had become cold, he had become hardened, and he had become...his father.

Justin finally goes in, to bed, and lies down beside Claire. He turns over, facing away from her, and closes his eyes, numb.

* * *

The following day, Mike Hardy receives the daily update from his assistant.

"Sir, that's it for the significant activities update."

"Thanks, Chris. I'll see you tomorrow."

Hardy's assistant doesn't leave.

"What is it?"

"Well sir, there is one more thing I need to brief you on. There was an unauthorized message broadcast yesterday. It was an internal broadcast, to a Phase Three employee, one of our new analysts that we hired a few months ago."

Hardy lets out a sigh and shakes his head.

"Let me guess. Tasha is still using Phase Three employees as her personal boy toys?"

"Do you want me to add this to the report, sir?"

Hardy sighs and shakes his head again.

"No. She will just find some way to justify it again to the old man, just like she did the last time."

"But sir, this makes three times in the past six weeks. If we don't..."

Hardy cuts him off as he turns back around from the door.

"Come on Chris, think about it. You don't think any other Society members are going to do this in the future, or worse? We have to catch her doing something 'illegal' within The Society laws, not immoral or unethical, but illegal. Just continue surveillance on her as normal. She'll slip up eventually. And when she does, we will have all of the evidence needed to finally get rid of her."

"Yes, sir."

* * *

The next few days go by and are somewhat slow and foggy for Justin. After not receiving anymore messages, he believes that the Tasha thing was probably just a one-time deal.

He's wrong.

That weekend, Justin receives another text message, requiring him to go over to Tasha's house once again. And, once again, he does whatever he has to do.

Over the next month, Justin received one or two messages a week, and it started becoming routine for him, just like everything else in his life.

Justin's initial anger about the situation quickly subsided. He became colder, heartless, more detached, and more like…Robert.

TWENTY-NINE

"Hello?" Robert answers the phone.

"Hey, it's me. I have another update to Hardy at the end of the month. We'll see what happens. That's not why I'm calling though. You know that other thing we talked about?

"Yeah, with Justin?"

"Yeah, that one. Well, it's become pretty regular now and, well, Justin has adapted to it. Not in a good way. And he has become pretty detached in the process."

"Do you think he'll stop working?"

"No, I'm not worried about him accomplishing the mission. But I am concerned about his morale, his wellbeing. I'm sure if he wasn't married he would be okay with this, this situation. But some of the things he told me that she has made him do to her, and what she has done to him…well it has to be hard on him. And he's not telling me that it's bothering him, but I can tell that it is. So I thought, maybe you could talk to him about it, get him to open up to you. You know, help him get some of this off his chest a little bit."

"Alright. I'll give him a call."

"How's Julia doing?"

"She's fine. She got held up in Georgia a little longer than we had planned, but so far she has convinced every contact to commit."

"And you?"

"And me what?"

"How are you holding up? I know you still haven't told her everything yet."

"I can't risk it right now. We are too close to the end to get emotional and lose focus. You let me worry about my parenting and you just worry about getting those files, before it's too late."

Robert hangs up the phone with Dr. Nichols, a little angered and upset from their conversation. He thinks about calling Justin, to try and help him.

Then he thinks about Julia, and how he still had to tell her the truth about Justin, and Brian. He quickly concludes that telling Julia over the phone is not a good idea.

Robert continues debating with himself about calling Justin. He figures that it could make things worse if he calls. And he figures that Justin would blame him for the situation he is in. So it is probably better to let Justin work it out on his own, and just stay focused on his mission. But is it worth it? To alienate him? To have Justin hate me, the same as Julia?

* * *

"Hello?"

"Hey, I just wanted to talk to you myself, and see how you were doing. It's been a while, Justin. So, how are you?"

"Why are you calling, Robert? I told Dr. Nichols I'm fine."

"Look, I've been where you are right now, Justin. The decisions you have to make and live with, and the secrets you have to keep from the ones you love. I've been there. I don't want you to end up like me, Justin. Or like Julia, and hating me."

"What are you saying?"

"If you want to stop, I can get you and your wife out of there, and into hiding. We can fabricate your deaths and get you somewhere safe. We can find another way to try and get intelligence from the inside of Hardy's department. I'm saying you can quit Justin. It's up to you."

There is a brief moment of silence on both ends. Justin feels the change in Robert's demeanor through his voice, and it actually gives him strength to hear the slight tone of compassion from him.

"Thanks for the call, and for the offer. I can't quit. I won't quit. Otherwise, everything that I have done will have been for nothing. You know, I see these people I work with every day, and they don't have any resemblance of freedom or happiness left. And then I think about my wife, and the rest of

America, the world, and I know I have to do something, to at least try. I'm going to do my part and see this thing through to the end Robert, for better or worse. Again, thanks for the call."

Robert puts down the phone and takes a drink.

He is relieved to hear what Justin said. But at the same time, he hates the fact that he is the one who put Justin in this situation at all.

Am I doing the right thing here? Robert asks himself.

After a few moments, he stops dwelling on it. He lights a cigarette and goes back to work on the map, plotting Julia's progress and updating her notes from the road.

THIRTY

Julia stares at the exit signs for Charlotte, North Carolina, as she passes them one by one on the highway.

She knew she could stop and see Brian if she wanted to, and nobody would know, her father wouldn't know. But she wasn't ready yet. She knew he was okay and that was enough to keep her going right now. That, and the fact she still didn't have a solid plan on how to get Brian out of there.

Everything was going fine on the road and her East Coast mission. And Julia wanted to keep it that way.

So, she keeps heading straight on the highway, passing the exit signs one by one. She continues straight on the highway to her next contact location, focused, and alone.

THIRTY-ONE

Robert comes home from work and sees Dr. Nichols' car, parked in the back of his house. He goes inside quickly, assuming something is wrong because of the unscheduled visit.

"Will, what's going on? What are you doing here? Is Justin okay? I just talked with him the other day."

"He's fine. We have another problem though. I had my update with Hardy this morning. It's not good Robert. They're going to start shipping out Phase Three injections next week, along with rapid scanners, based on my prototype."

Robert almost stops breathing for a second, his veins tingling with adrenalin and his face pulsating with anxiety.

"Did you find out why?"

"The only thing I came up with, based off Justin's intel, is that they are worried about some of the Society members trying to move up and expand ownership amongst other factions. I met with Mr. Hardy, Senior, a while back, and there were a lot of curious Inner Circle members in his office that day. I didn't catch on to it at first, but then Justin saw the increase in the international Society leaders under surveillance. Apparently, there has been some division within the ranks between some of the major countries, and sides were quietly being taken. There were some wiretaps that picked up on a possible regime change of the Hardy dynasty. That's all we know for now. How many contacts does Julia have left to meet?"

"There's no time for that now, Will. I've got to get her back here. We're going to have to go with what we have now, and hope that it's enough. We have to get Justin out too."

"Give me a few more days, Robert. That's all I'm asking for. I'm going to get those files on the main server. I can take greater risks now because of this timeline. If we don't get them now, then we will never get another chance like this. And without those files, our chance to stop The Society permanently goes out the window and we may never know how the messaging works."

Robert lights a cigarette and contemplates the idea for a moment.

"Three days, Will. I'll give you three more days and then I'm pulling you out, both of you."

"Okay. I'll get them, Robert. I promise. I won't let you down."

* * *

Robert calls Dave Sweeney first, and gives him a heads up. He confirms everything is ready in the bunker and the cabin.

Robert calls Julia next, to have her start spreading the word to all of the contacts that are committed, and to update them on the expedited timeline. He finishes briefing her the update on the phone.

Julia was in receive-mode during his brief and he was now waiting for her to say something, anything.

"I'm bringing Brian back with me."

"Julia, I don't…"

"I don't care what you have to say about it, and I don't need your permission. You might be able to turn your back on him, on us. But I can't, and I won't."

"Julia, let me finish. I tried to tell you this before, but I couldn't. But now I have to tell you, you have to know. Brian is…Brian is not my son, Julia…he's not my blood."

He pauses for a moment. Julia remains silent, upset and shocked about what he has been waiting so long to tell her.

"Your mom got pregnant with him while we were having, problems, when I was retiring. You can't help him Julia, he's not immune like we are. He's already infected with Phase Two. I'm sorry to do this over the phone, Julia. It's not how I played this conversation out in my head, over and over again."

He pauses again, and once again Julia remains quiet, with utter disbelief.

"And Justin...Justin is my real son. The woman you asked about in the picture was his mother. She died giving birth to him. And then I gave him up for adoption, immediately after. I never wanted to tell you like this. But, whatever happens now, you know everything. That's it, that's all of it, no more lies between us."

Julia wipes her face.

"I don't care. I don't care, Brian is still my brother. And, I love him, and I am going to get him. He still has a chance to live some kind of life. He's not Phase Three yet."

"Julia..."

"I'm finished, okay. Even though I hate you for what you did to me, and for the man you have become over the years...I will 'always' love you, because you are my father. And well Dad, that's just how family is supposed to be. Bye."

Robert tries calling back and the phone just rings. He struggles with himself over whether or not he made the right decision telling her. And he wonders if he will ever see her again.

* * *

Dr. Nichols goes to work at his lab the next day. He paces in his office all morning, waiting for noon to come so he could make his move.

Ten minutes until twelve on the clock. He begins walking, making his way to see Hardy.

He enters the surveillance and targeting department and is escorted by security to Hardy's office. He sees Mike Hardy and his assistant through the glass windows, getting ready to leave for lunch. He knocks on the door.

"I'm sorry, Dr. Nichols. Can you come back later? Mr. Hardy is off to a lunch meeting."

Dr. Nichols sits his briefcase down and quickly pulls out some papers.

"Yeah, umm…here, I just wanted to give you these updated designs on the scanners that you asked for, sir."

The assistant takes the papers from him and puts them in his folder.

"Great. I'll take a look at them this afternoon. Thanks, Will."

"Sure, no problem. Thank you, sir."

Dr. Nichols stands in front of the door, and he stares at the clock on the wall behind Hardy.

"Okay then. Was there something else, Will?

"Umm…well actually…"

The fire alarm goes off and lights on the wall start blinking.

"Come on sir, let's get you out of here. You're going to be late."

Dr. Nichols walks out with them and stops at the department exit doors.

"Sir, I left my briefcase. It's got my new prototype software in it. I'll just be a second."

"I'll go back with him Mr. Hardy."

"No, Chris. It's okay. You left my door open anyways. Go pull my car around. I'm not going to be any later to my father's meeting because of another false alarm. This is the third fire alarm in the past week." Hardy smiles at Dr. Nichols and begins walking away. "Oh, and Will, shut my door on the way out please."

"Yes, sir."

Dr. Nichols gets inside Hardy's office and closes the door. He looks out the office windows and every employee is exiting, and all cameras have been tilted to the exit doors. He makes his move and plugs in a small USB to the back of Hardy's computer. He connects a remote access wire from the computer to a handheld tablet. He quickly types in codes and uploads the backdoor program from the USB. He sees a security team enter the main department doors and he ducks under the desk.

"Come on, come on." He whispers.

The screen blinks green on the tablet. He unplugs the remote access wire and fumbles for the USB. He sees the guards walking around the windows and toward Hardy's office door. His fingers get a grip on the USB and he jerks. Crack. He grabs a small handful of plastic USB pieces on the carpet and hurries back to his briefcase, across the room. He looks up at the guard, standing over him at the door.

"Are you injured, sir?"

"No. No, I'm just grabbing my briefcase."

"Please evacuate the building, sir."

Dr. Nichols walks out quickly and heads straight toward his lab. He accesses the main server and starts downloading the files to a disk. A lab security guard startles him at his computer.

"Please evacuate the building, sir. There is a fire alarm, sir."

"Yeah, sure. I'm almost done here."

The guard stands there, waiting for him to leave.

The files are all encrypted. He would have to decrypt them at home with his personal software. He imagined how long it would take.

The guard walks closer to him. "Sir, if you do not leave I must use force to escort you out. There is a fire alarm, sir."

"Okay, okay. Look, I'm done. See, I'm leaving, okay?"

The files finish downloading. He pulls out the disk, brushes past the guard and then rushes home. He calls Robert but there is no answer.

* * *

"Chris, grab Dr. Nichols for me. I looked over these designs, but I have some questions about them."

Hardy's assistant leaves the office and goes to the lab, looking around for Dr. Nichols. He can't find him. He stops one of the lab security guards.

"Where's Dr. Nichols?"

"He left during the fire alarm, sir."

"Okay. Wait, where did you see him leaving from?"

"From his office, sir."

"And this was during the alarm?"

"Yes, sir."

"What was he doing?"

"He was on his computer, sir."

Hardy's assistant leaves the lab and goes back to the surveillance department, suspicious of Dr. Nichol's actions.

"Pull up the computer logs for Dr. Nichols, and then show me the CCTV on the lab and his house for the past two hours." Chris says to an analyst.

Chris looks at the screen and then at the computer logs of Dr. Nichols. He scrolls down and sees what he accessed during the alarm. He sprints into Hardy's office.

"Sir, we have a problem! Dr. Nichols accessed the main server. He accessed the restricted files and now he's gone. Our cameras have him at his house right now. What do you want to do, sir?"

"How did he get access?" Hardy thinks for a moment. "The briefcase? Bring him in. I want to find out what he's doing immediately. And get me all of the second and third-party contact files on him."

Hardy walks over to his assistant and places his hands firmly on the man's shoulders.

"Chris, I want to contain this quietly, and quickly, before I have to brief my father. Understood?"

"Yes sir, I'm on it."

The assistant gets a team dispatched to apprehend Dr. Nichols at his house.

Justin sees the commotion from his desk and knows that something is wrong. He goes to the bathroom, out of routine, and changes the SIM card on his phone.

He calls Dr. Nichols. No answer. He calls his house phone.

"Hello?"

"It's me, Justin."

"What are doing calling me on this number? Call me back on the cell."

Justin hangs up and then calls him back on the other phone. He peeks out of the stall to make sure he is still alone in the bathroom.

"What is it, Justin?"

"Something's wrong here. People are running around, and a squad of field agents are deploying right now. I don't know where they are going but I think you should run. Did you get the files?"

He looks at his computer and only two of the files have been decrypted.

"Yeah! I got the files kid! But I still don't know what they are yet. Alright, just keep tabs on where that team is headed, and I'm going to get out of here soon. And tell Robert I'm headed his way. We did it kid, we really did it! I'll see you later."

Justin tries calling Robert but there's no answer. The bathroom door opens, and Justin quickly flushes the toilet, and then returns to his desk.

He looks at the clock. He still has more than two hours left on his shift.

* * *

Dr. Nichols looks at his watch and then at the computer. He pours a drink to celebrate and opens the two files that were decrypted already.

He begins reading.

Finally, the answers to their questions and The Society's darkest secrets were now right in front of him. The moment was surreal. He couldn't believe what he was reading, and that was only two files worth.

He finishes his drink and starts packing a small bag while the other files continue decrypting.

He zips the side of his bag after he finishes packing and then he hears multiple car doors shut. He looks out his window and sees a dozen or more AGI agents walking toward his house. He runs back to his computer room and attaches all of the files in an email and hits send. He closes his computer slowly, knowing he would never see the end of his and Robert's plan to stop The Society. He walks slowly back to the kitchen and pours another drink, filling the glass all the way to the top.

A loud knocking begins at the front door.

"Dr. Nichols! Please open the door, sir! You will have thirty seconds to open the door sir, and then we will enter with force!"

He knew he could not be taken back to AGI alive. He knew what they would do to him to get the truth, about him, about everything.

He walks over to his alarm system panel and punches in a series of numbers. He then inputs '30' and strikes enter. He takes a seat on the couch and looks over at a photo of his son on the counter in front of him, and then slams the drink in one shot. He picks up the photo and holds it in front of him.

The front and back doors both burst open.

"Hello boys. Looks like you made it just in time for the show."

"Secure the doctor. Protector Main, this is agent Two-Bravo, we have the…"

Boom! Boom! Boom!

The house blows up in a series of large, sequential explosions. Fire, smoke, and debris darken the clear, afternoon sky. Sounds of chaos ring out through the quiet, residential neighborhood.

* * *

Justin's shift is finally up.

He leaves as fast as he can without looking suspicious. As he gets closer to his home, he notices smoke protruding above the neighborhood near Dr. Nichols' house, just a few miles from his exit.

"No, come on, please."

Justin breaks routine and drives past the street where Dr. Nichols' house used to be. Now, Justin stares with heartache at a small crumbled pile of blackened bricks, random wood and debris, and smoke, smoke bellowing up from all of it.

THIRTY-TWO

Robert carefully exits the boiler room area of his hospital, making his final round of inspections on the bombs he had wired throughout the night.

It wasn't a high value target, compared to some of the other facilities on their list, but it was still an AGI owned facility. And there were three, somewhat high ranking, Society members that worked there. It would still be a small victory for them.

He gets in his car and drives home for the day. He sees all of the missed calls on his phone. He tries calling Justin and Dr. Nichols back with no luck.

Robert arrives home and heads straight to the basement. He turns on all of the television screens and computers, and then pours a drink, as his normal routine. Most of the screens are showing similar images and video footage of a house on fire. He turns up the volume.

- ...and emergency services have put out the fire now and have confirmed the death of multiple AGI employees. Of those confirmed dead include the homeowner, Dr. William Nichols of AGI Headquarters, here in Washington, D.C. And it appears to have been ruled as an electrical fire accident. We can't release the names of the others that have been confirmed dead, but we expect to have those within the hour. Now, to move on to other breaking -

Robert mutes the TV and grips the desk in anger, in pain.

His phone rings.

"Justin?"

"No, it's me. I'm sorry. I just heard on the radio."

"Julia? I didn't expect to hear from you, after the way our last conversation ended. Are you okay? Where are you?"

"Yeah, I'm okay. I'm still driving, back south, to get Brian."

Robert avoids starting an argument or trying to convince her about Brian.

"I haven't heard from Justin yet, Julia. And I'm worried. It's only a matter of time now before they find out about him, and me, us. They will investigate Dr. Nichols and trace him to us. Look, I know it's a lot to ask, but Justin might need some help getting out of there, Julia."

"I am not backtracking that many hours, just to help him get out of there. He's a grown man, Brian is just a kid! Are you kidding me right now? Brian needs my help more than Justin does, whether he's infected or not."

"Julia…"

Julia hangs up the phone and pulls over.

I am not going back, she says to herself. He is a grown man. He was in the military for crying out loud. No, he can take care of himself. Satisfied with her rationalization, she starts to pull off.

She stops the car.

Having another person to help me get Brian would be nice though, she says, in case something goes wrong. He is my brother too, just as much blood as Brian. And Brian is not in any immediate danger right now.

She looks at the clock on the dash. There's still enough time to turn around right now and save them both, she rationalizes again. She slams the steering wheel in frustration and looks in the rearview mirror for a moment.

Julia puts the car in reverse and does a U-turn.

THIRTY-THREE

Mike Hardy looks across at Tasha. She looks back with a crooked smile on her face. He knows she is embellishing in this moment.

The door opens up and Mr. Hardy walks in, and the two of them stand up.

"Have a seat. I've been briefed on the details of this 'Nichols' situation already. So, here is what is going to happen. Tasha, your network department is going to work hand in hand with Mike's targeting and surveillance department. We are going to target, and eliminate, all second and third-party contacts of Dr. Nichols. I'm getting pressure from the board, and the circle, to contain this as fast as possible, using whatever means necessary."

"Sir, I…"

"It's not up for discussion, Mike. Now, get to work and brief me when you are done and when we are complete. You have forty-eight hours. Press releases will need to read as accidental deaths for any of their high-profile relationships. Now get it done."

Mr. Hardy leaves the office. Tasha looks at Mike.

"Well, it looks like I get a chance to run Phase Two messaging on large scale after all, Michael."

Mike Hardy gets up angry and walks out.

"And don't worry Michael, I'll make it quick for them."

He continues walking away, without saying anything.

THIRTY-FOUR

"Hello? Justin?" Robert asks.

"Yeah, it's me."

"I've been calling nonstop. Where are you?"

"I'm home. I'm okay."

"You're not okay, Justin. You have to get out of there. It won't be long before they find out about me, then you."

"I was planning on leaving tonight. And I'm bringing my wife. I know what you are going to say, but I would rather have this version of her than nothing at all."

"Okay. I won't say anything. Stick to as many small roads as possible."

"I'm sorry about Dr. Nichols. I know you two were close. He was a good man. And you're not going to believe it, but he got the files out, Robert. Too bad we won't ever know what was on them though. But he did what he said he would do, he got the files."

"Are you sure he got the files out?"

"Yeah, positive. He probably told me three times on the phone, before he died. He was definitely proud and excited about it."

"I've got to go, Justin. Be safe, okay. And keep your wife away from the TV, radios, phones, anything electronic. She's Phase Two and she is still susceptible to receiving messages from AGI."

"Will do."

Robert hangs up and logs in an Email account.

He sees one new message. He opens it.

Robert smiles, and then folds his head on the desk, bittersweet happiness.

* * *

Justin walks to the living room and turns off the television.

He looks at his wife and pulls the phone out of her hand. "Hey, I've got an idea. Let's go on a vacation. What do you think?"

"No. It's not vacation season yet."

"I know, but there is a new vacation season now, a new one that just started. You just haven't heard about it yet. They told me about it at work."

"Okay. Where are we going?"

"Let's just start packing for now and I'll tell you on the way there, okay?"

"I need to post on my page anytime I go on vacation or leave the area though."

"Yeah, sure. We'll do that later though, okay?"

"Okay."

* * *

"Mr. Hardy. Sir, you need to take a look at this. There was an incoming call to his home phone, just minutes before the explosion."

"And?"

"Well, look. The call originated from this building, sir. AGI Headquarters. The number is untraceable though, probably a burner phone."

"So, there's someone else on the inside that was working with him? Lockdown the building, Chris. And search everyone, I mean everyone. Go through all of the CCTV from today in the building, and exploit anything out of the ordinary."

"Yes, sir."

Hardy's assistant gets the entire surveillance department started on the tasks.

* * *

Tasha walks into Hardy's office, unannounced and with open access now.

"This is fun, isn't it? Working together. I've already executed four successful kill missions using Phase Two messaging."

"What do you want, Tasha? I'm busy."

Hardy's assistant walks in and interrupts them.

"Sir, we found something."

Hardy gets up and walks past Tasha, following his assistant to the big screen in the middle of the surveillance department.

A photo of Justin appears on the screen.

Hardy looks at the photo and then back at Tasha. He watches as the smile disappears from her face, and she watches Hardy's smile get larger and larger.

"Justin Brown. A somewhat recent hire. He came on during our rapid expansion last quarter. Well he made an unusual, and somewhat longer, bathroom break today sir. Right after we launched the team to get Dr. Nichols. We pulled the audio feed from the bathroom."

Justin's voice and phone conversation starts playing on the speaker.

Hardy looks back at Tasha again.

She puts her head down and walks out of the room.

"Alright, that's enough. Great work, Chris. Great work. Move him up on the list and get a message package out to his wife, right away. Have a field team on standby as well. This Justin Brown is either not infected, or he's being controlled by someone else in the Society, other than us here at headquarters. I need to go brief the old man on these updates."

"Yes sir, I'll have a team ready to go and we'll get the message package out shortly."

Mike Hardy walks in his father's office, and he sees that Tasha has already beaten him there.

Tasha wipes her eyes as he enters and then leaves the office. She slightly winks at Hardy as she passes, just enough for him to see what she did.

"What is it, Mike?"

"What did Tasha have to say?"

"Well for one, she told me about her sexual misuse of a Phase Three employee."

"It's more than just one. And the one she told you about is not Phase Three."

"Well, she told me that too."

"So, she's finished then, right?"

"Look Mike, we need to do what's best for The Society here, what's best for America, and 'Our' future. I don't need one of my top executives being brought down on top of this, this disaster of a situation. A situation in which your department was involved in, need I remind you. It was your guys that hired this infiltrator, Mike. Remember that."

Mr. Hardy walks over and places a hand on his son's shoulder.

"You are my son, Mike, and I want you take my place at the top one day. Don't make that impossible for me to do, okay? Now, you need let this thing go with Tasha, so you can do what Michael Hardy 'Junior' needs to do, to take over one day.

"Yes, sir."

* * *

Mike Hardy walks around his surveillance department and finds his assistant.

"Where are we at, Chris?"

"Messages have been sent out, sir. And we have a team headed there right now, as backup, in case the messages fail."

"Pull up the CCTV from the house on the big screen again."

"We've been monitoring it sir, but everything still looks to be normal routine."

"Wait, say that again."

"We've been monitoring it, sir? But, everything still looks to be normal routine?"

"Exactly. That's it, Chris. That's the problem."

"Excuse me, sir? I don't understand what you mean."

"He shouldn't be acting normal right now. Think about it. He was involved with Dr. Nichols, right? And he has to know Dr. Nichols is dead by now. It's been all over the news for hours now."

Hardy stops talking and stares at something on the screen for a second.

"That's it, right there. Zoom in on the TV in their living room, right there. Do you see it? Look at the news. Now look at the news on our TV. It's a loop, Chris. Get that entry team to his house, quick."

* * *

"Okay, I think I've packed everything we need."

Justin checks the bedroom. "Sweetie?"

He walks into the kitchen. Empty.

He tries their study room next and sees the computer screen open with her social media page displayed.

"Sweetie? Claire? Where are you? We need to talk for a second, honey."

He turns around and his wife lunges at him out of the darkness, her hand raised and brandishing a large kitchen knife. He blocks it out of natural reflex and they wrestle each other to the ground.

"Stop! Stop it!" Justin screams to his wife, trying to gain control of the knife.

They roll around on the floor for a moment. Justin pries the knife loose and throws it across the floor. She punches him hard in the head and starts going for the knife. Justin makes it to his feet and starts out the door.

As he takes a step, he feels a sharp pain in his upper back, near his shoulder blade. He feels the cold blade slide through his flesh, scraping across bones, and it takes his breath away by surprise. He then feels her hand latch on the back of his neck, and then he feels the knife again, being ripped out this time, fast and hard.

Without thinking, Justin picks up a small brass sculpture from the desk and smashes it square against his wife's face, shattering bone and flesh. Her head and body bounces off the wall and then onto the ground from the tremendous force of Justin's blow.

Justin stares at her body in a daze for a few minutes, trying to comprehend what just happened. Justin touches the back of his shoulder and gasps in pain from the stab wound.

"Claire?"

He kicks the knife across the room and bends down by her side. He gently lifts her head from the ground and into his lap.

There was fresh blood everywhere, puddles on the floor and sprayed like paint across the wall. Justin had hit her clean across her temple.

He felt no heartbeat, no breath.

Just like that, he had killed her.

No time to mourn, Justin kisses her forehead and gently lays her head back down. He fumbles his way back to the kitchen and pours a drink, and then another. He tries to bandage the wound with his left hand as best he could.

He sets the drink down and sees three sets of headlights coming up his street.

Justin never found the time to wire the house with explosives, like Dr. Nichols had told him to do before, after Justin first moved in. He only had a couple of explosives, and they were crudely placcd underneath the living room floor in the house. There were no detonators, no wires, and no trigger mechanisms. He would have to blow them manually.

He pulls an aerosol can out of a cabinet, along with bottles of cooking oil, lighter fluid, anything remotely flammable he could find. He empties them on the carpet, then the curtains, and then the floor leading to the back door. He pulls up a few of the hardwood tiles, exposing the explosives that were underneath, just sitting there.

Justin moves back, to the back door, and then torches the trail of liquid on the floor leading to the explosives. He watches the fire jump and dance, into the living room and then onto the curtains, right above the explosives.

Justin takes one last look at his wife, lifeless, covered in blood, and then he runs off into the woods.

* * *

"Sir, the team is standing by, at the house."

"Good. Let me know when he's dead."

"Yes, sir."

"Wait," the analyst adjusts his earpiece. "What was that?...One-Charlie, say again...Can you still enter?...Well try then."

"Sir, the team can see flames in the windows. They think they can still enter though. Apparently, the fire is not that big."

"Pull up their body cams and audio feed on the big screen."

Hardy watches the team clear the house, room by room, bypassing the fire in the living room. Claire Brown's body appears on the screen.

"One confirmed dead. I repeat, the wife is confirmed dead. Charlie Team continuing the search for the husband."

"Wait! Chris did you see that?"

"What's that, sir?"

"That trail of fire leading to the back door. Why would there be a trail of fire like that? Get them out of there now! He's not trying to burn it down, he's trying to blow it up, like Dr. Nichols did!"

"All teams abort immediately! I repeat, abort!"

The team exits quickly and makes it back to their vehicles.

A few minutes go by. Nothing.

"Well, I feel kind of stupid here, Chris. I guess I was wrong. Get a bomb team out there just in case though. And get a bird in the air. I want the teams on the ground to start combing the area for him. He can't be that far away yet, if he got away.

THIRTY-FIVE

Julia is having a hard time reading the street signs through the rain.

She pulls over and opens her notes to verify Justin's address.

A loud boom startles her.

She looks in the sky, first thinking it was a large lighting strike, but there was no thunder that followed. She looks over the forest of trees and sees a fiery cloud, slowly rising in the air. She knows she is in the vicinity of Justin's neighborhood and house. She thinks that she is too late. Either The Society killed him, or he killed himself like Dr. Nichols, she thinks, in order to protect everyone else involved.

She puts the car in gear and begins to slowly drive off, feeling remorse for not being able to help him.

She gasps and slams on the brakes.

Justin's face appears near her window and his hand smacks her front windshield. Small trails of blood flow from his hand and mix with the rain, rolling down the edge of the windshield.

"Julia…" Justin exhales out with exhaustion.

Julia quickly unlocks the passenger door and Justin slides inside, falling into the seat.

Julia reaches across and closes the door for him.

"Justin! I thought, I thought you were dead. I just saw the explosion."

"Go, go…we need to put as much distance between us as possible. They're going to find out, ah…that I made it out alive."

Julia quickly accelerates down the road and on to the highway.

"Ahh!"

Justin leans forward, and Julia sees all of the blood on his back and shoulder, and what looks like a deep stab wound. She sees the poor job of his self-bandage attempt. His left hand is cut up as well.

"You're bleeding pretty good there. What happened?" Julia asks, while reaching behind him and then handing him one of her shirts from the backseat. She opens the middle console and then hands him a bottle of pain pills with her bottle of water.

Justin takes the shirt and wraps his hand quietly. He takes a handful of the pills and then looks out his window. He tilts his head back into the seat and closes his eyes.

"I don't know, Julia. I can't explain it."

Julia looks over at him. The blood. No mention of his wife. She knows what happened.

"Once we get out of state, I'll stop and re-dress your wounds. Just hang on a little bit until then."

* * *

Justin wakes up in a small bed, with fresh bandages on his hand and back.

He sees an older gentleman sitting in a chair, looking right at him and smoking a cigar.

He looks around the room but can't find Julia.

"Julia?"

"Relax there killer. She's outside, on the phone with Robert."

"Who are you?"

"Me? I'm just a friend of Robert's." He takes a puff from the cigar. "And a friend of yours, now. You lost a good amount of blood, but you'll be alright. A little sore and weak maybe, but you'll live."

Justin notices the blood stains on the old man's hands, as he smokes the cigar.

"Thanks. Whatever your name is."

Julia walks in and looks at Justin.

"How do you feel?"

"Like I've been stabbed. Other than that, okay I guess."

"Boyd, can you give us a minute?"

The man nods and walks outside.

Julia waits for him to leave and then pulls the chair close to Justin, and sits down beside him.

She looks at him for a moment, thinking to herself. Tall. Handsome. Well-built muscular frame. Strong face but still welcoming. And those eyes, those familiar eyes. Appearing to almost change colors at times, from hazel to blue. Why didn't I recognize it before? Why couldn't I see it? How we look alike and how he resembles, Robert.

She thinks about Brian for a brief second. Brian looked nothing like the two of them, a little like her mother, but not like her or Justin.

"So, I'm guessing you knew I was your sister for a while, and Robert asked you not to tell me?"

"Julia, I…"

"Let me finish. Even though I don't really know you, you're my brother, just as much as Brian is. And I'm not going to die, knowing that I turned my back on either one of you. So, now that you owe me, you are going to help me. You're going to help me get Brian, 'Our' brother."

Julia leans back in the chair. Justin doesn't argue.

"Good. Now, we don't have a lot of time to spare. I'll get you something to eat and then we have to hit the road."

Julia gets up and walks to the door.

"Thank you, Julia. Thank you for coming back. And I'm sorry. I should have told you, instead of keeping Robert's secrets."

Julia pauses at the door and turns. She looks at Justin and relaxes her eyes at him, her brother.

* * *

"Well?"

"Nothing yet Mr. Hardy, we're still searching, sir. The wife is the only body we found in the house. Nothing from the road blocks or air traffic yet. We do know that he is injured though, sir. We found his blood at the entrance of the woods, but then the rain made it impossible to keep track after that."

"Chris, if you do not find him, or his dead body, within the next twelve hours, then your chance of immunity will, without-a-doubt, be in jeopardy. Do I make myself clear?"

"Yes, sir. Clear, sir."

THIRTY-SIX

"Hello?"

"Ian, it's me. Is this line clean?

"Robert? Yeah, it's clean. What are you doing calling me? I thought I was just going through Julia, to be safer."

"I need a personal favor, that's why I'm calling you direct. I promised Will I would make sure his son was taken care of, if anything happened to him. Well, I need to make good on my promise now. But I need your help to do that, for me. I just don't have the time to make it there. As you know, our plans have changed."

"Is he, well, infected?"

"No, he's immune. That's another reason I need to make sure we secure him, on top of the promise."

"I'm assuming he's at Will's first home address?"

"Yeah, his old address near you. Look, I'm sorry it came to this, with Phase Three, with everything. I thought we had a real chance."

"It's not your fault, Robert. We can still fight them. I'll still fight them."

"Thanks Ian, and good luck brother."

Robert hangs up and finishes packing some essential computer gear, maps, and files from the basement. He takes one last look at the basement from the top of the stairs, thinking about all of the years spent planning in that room.

All those years, spent planning on how to stop The Society from succeeding with the TSOMBIE program. All those years, just to come so close, and then fail. It was heartbreaking to him. Regardless of the odds against them, Robert always believed that they had a real chance to succeed. He believed it was destiny to stop them.

He turns out the light and closes the door.

Robert finishes loading his car and sets the security alarm on his house.

He takes one last look at the house, and then he gets in his car and begins driving. And thinking, thinking about his new home and new life, of living underground.

* * *

The sun rises along the highway.

Robert thinks about all of the little things that he has taken for granted over the years, knowing that America was about to change, permanently change, forever. He thinks about being immune and begins to think that maybe it is a curse instead of a blessing.

He looks at other drivers on the highway as he passes them, soon to be infected with Phase Three with no living consciousness, no freedom. And he thinks, ignorance is truly bliss.

At least they would never be aware of the freedom, the freedom they once had. At least they would never be aware of the freedom, the freedom they would never have.

THIRTY-SEVEN

Tasha McNeil and Mike Hardy sit in silence in the conference room, along with all of the other board members.

Mr. Hardy walks in and takes a seat at the head of the table.

"Good morning everyone. Let's begin, shall we?"

A senior board member and department director begins briefing.

"Sir, members of the board, all of the Phase Three shipments have gone out, and about eighty percent are already at their final destinations. The media campaign has effectively communicated Phase Three as a necessary vaccination, for an out-of-season epidemic strand of Type A flu, called 'T2020.' Our numbers indicate we are a go to start injections as planned, within the next twenty-four hours. We have no concerns at this time.'"

The board member sits down, and Mike Hardy begins speaking.

"Rapid TSOMBIE scanners have been issued to all AGI, Society owned facilities. After seventy-two hours of injections, local and international teams will begin conducting screenings in all major cities. Mass implementation of rapid scanners will also begin in all public buildings and transportation facilities. We have no concerns at this time."

Tasha looks at Mike and then begins her brief.

"Phase Three basic message packages have been disseminated to all Society members. Personalized packages are still available, for premium cost, but they can be tailored to better meet your professional or personal demands. All within the mandated, national and international Society laws, of course. We have no concerns at this time."

Mr. Hardy closes his folder and looks at the group, from his head seat at the table.

"Tomorrow will be another monumental day in this great nation's history, and I would like to personally thank everyone for all of their hard work, and dedication. And just to quell any rumors out there, thanks to my team here at AGI Headquarters, I can assure you that the 'Nichols' situation has been taken care of, rest assured. Now…let's start celebrating!"

Everyone stands and claps. Casual conversations and congratulations begin amongst all of the members in the room.

"Tasha, Mike, please join me in my office."

They both shake hands with other members as they leave the conference room and follow Mr. Hardy to his office.

He closes the door after they come in.

"Okay, now don't make me a liar out there. Where do we stand?"

"Sir, thirty of the thirty-eight known contacts of Dr. Nichols have been taken out by Phase Two kill messages."

"Impressive Tasha, but that's not what I want to hear. Mike, I want you to quit the subtle tactics. Start conducting full-out raids on their locations and get this over with. No more messages. It's effective, but it's taking too long. I want all of the people he was connected with confirmed dead, before we start injections. And Tasha, I want you to go back to your department and focus on Phase Three messages. Let Mike finish this."

Mike Hardy grins to himself, before they both respond.

"Yes, sir."

"Yes, sir."

THIRTY-EIGHT

Justin wakes up in the passenger seat. The car engine cutting off wakes him to a quiet, suburb scene.

He looks over at Julia. She is staring at something intensely. He sits up.

"How long was I out?"

"A while."

"Sorry, those pills work pretty good. Are we already there?"

"Yeah. That's the house. Third one on the left."

"You still going through with the same crazy plan? The one you talked about earlier?"

"Yep, straight through the front door."

"When?"

Julia gets out of the car and starts making a beeline for the house.

"Okay, I guess that means now."

Justin gets out and into the driver seat. He rolls the car slowly down the street behind her, toward the entrance of the driveway.

Julia rings the doorbell. Trent's new wife answers the door. Julia stares at her.

"Yes, may I help you?"

Julia looks at her and how pretty she is, how young.

"I'm here to get Brian. I'm not leaving without him, so just let me in."

"And you are?"

"Julia. Brian's sister."

The woman's head tilts a little and twitches slightly.

"I don't understand. Brian's sister is dead, I'm sorry, thank you for stopping by."

She starts closing the door and Julia pushes it back open, hard, and takes her down to the ground. The two wrestle for a moment and then Julia gains positive control of her hands and pulls a set of zip ties from behind her back, securing her quickly.

Julia stands up and sees a figure step out at the corner of the hallway.

"Brian? Hey buddy, it's me, I came back to get you. You need to come with me now. It's not safe here Brian, we need to leave, okay?"

"Who are you? What did you do to Amanda?"

"Brian, it's me, Julia…your sister."

She starts walking toward him and he takes a step back. Brian tilts his head.

"My sister is dead. Amanda?"

"Brian, call the police."

Brian turns and moves toward the stairs.

Julia runs a couple of steps and grabs him.

"Come on Brian, we have to go now." Julia grabs his arms tight and starts pulling him toward the door.

"Let go of me."

Brian breaks free near the door and runs outside, straight into Justin. Justin zip ties him on the ground.

"Don't hurt him, Justin."

A kid riding a bicycle stops at the driveway. "What are you doing to Brian?"

"Let's go. Get him in the car. We have to get out of here."

They get him in the backseat and jump in. Justin sits in the back and Julia gets behind the wheel, flooring the accelerator.

"Who are you? I don't understand. My sister is dead."

"It's going to be okay buddy. You're safe now. We're not going to hurt you." Justin tries to touch him, and he backs away.

Julia looks at Justin in the rearview mirror with watery eyes, and then focuses back on the road and the drive ahead. Everything is going to be okay now, she thinks to herself. We're all going to be okay now, together.

THIRTY-NINE

Robert ditches his car, deep in the woods and several miles away from the cabin. He then begins his walk to the cabin.

He pulls out his compass a few times to stay on course, and after a couple of hours of hiking, he makes it.

Dave happens to be outside at the moment, and sees Robert coming out of the tree line.

He greets him at the back porch. "Here, let me help you."

Dave grabs one of the bags from Robert and sits it down. They share a brief hug.

"Good to see you, Robert. Not under these conditions, but still good to see you."

"Thanks, you too. And everything is ready in the bunker?"

"Absolutely. I ran the normal weekly checks on the air filtration and the generators a few days ago, no issues. It took me over a month, but I finally have the camera cable buried and ran into the bunker, so we can monitor the cabin. Have you heard from Julia yet?

"No, not yet."

"What about the contacts?"

"There were a few we couldn't convince, but we have more than have enough to still disrupt The

Society. Even if it is brief, it will still stir up some doubt amongst them, and give the uninfected hope to survive. Amy and the baby?"

"Doing great. Amy's not looking forward to leaving the cabin, but they're doing fine. My little girl is walking everywhere now. She's a lot bigger since the last time you seen her. I've got a full-course dinner almost ready, last meal and all. Sorry, that wasn't really funny."

"No, not really. Yeah, let's go inside though."

FORTY

Mike comes out of the coffee lounge and sees a group of Society members, all huddled around one of the TV screens. He takes a closer look and sees aerial views of a house fire. He recognizes the name, Dr. Singer. He runs back to his department and finds his assistant.

"What the hell is this, Chris?"

"Sir, one of our raid teams just made entry into a third-party contact of Dr. Nichols, a Dr. Singer in Tennessee. And then the house blew up, as soon as they entered. It was rigged with explosives, just like the other one."

"Well get it off the news! Now! And start a deep dive on Dr. Singer!"

Mike Hardy leaves the department, infuriated, knowing that he had to go and brief his father.

* * *

Mike Hardy returns to his office from a harsh, one-sided briefing.

Hardy's assistant is sitting in his office when he gets back.

"What did you find out?"

"Well, it's not good sir, it goes deeper than we thought."

He lays out a folder with pictures of Justin Brown and Dr. Singer, side by side.

"Captain Justin Brown was a patient of his before we hired him. Singer's wife died while giving birth to their son and then Singer gave the son up for adoption, on the same day. It's the same birthday as Justin Brown. The records on file were forged, but we finally tracked down the originals. According to Dr. Singer's records, he came to America from Germany in the early 90's, and began working at an AGI hospital in Nashville, Tennessee, shortly after arriving. He specialized in treating veterans. We're going through all of his patient records at the hospital now to verify, but we think he may have more people helping him with, whatever it is, he is doing. But we think that his records may be forged as well, like Brown's."

"Gee, you think?" Hardy says sarcastically. He takes a moment and thinks about what to do, and calms down.

"Okay, this is what we're going to do. Begin surveillance on the most frequent and recent patients he had over the years. But keep this extremely close hold until we find out what kind of scale we are dealing with here. Other than that, there's nothing we can do about this now. There's no way I am bringing this to my father right now, the day before we implement Phase Three. And certainly not after my last conversation with him. He's already too paranoid and upset about the other events that have happened. Keep me updated and briefed by the hour on this, Chris."

"Yes, sir."

Mike Hardy closes his office door. He looks out into his department full of analysts, plugging mindlessly away at their computers, like the zombies they are.

He thinks about Dr. Singer and Justin Brown, and if this was the end of them, or if they did have more helping them. So what? He thinks to himself. It's too late, Phase Three is already out there. There's no stopping us now. We're going to be fine, he says to himself, I'm going to be fine. And the Hardy family alone is about to control everything, once and for all.

FORTY-ONE

Dave laughs with Amy. They laugh at their daughter running around the living room, playing.

Dave sees Robert lighting a cigarette on the back porch, the lighter flickering in the night, through the window.

"I'll be back in a minute."

Dave grabs a half-empty bottle of whiskey from the table and walks outside.

Robert is sitting on the steps, looking up at the sky.

"Still nothing?"

Robert shakes his head. "They should be here by now."

Dave offers him a drink. Robert shakes his head again. Dave is surprised at the refusal. He takes a small drink by himself.

"Maybe we should have put a moon roof in the bunker? I'm really going to miss the sky. I've only been in there a few hours at a time, and I still can't see how Julia survived that long down there. All by herself down there, without giving up, all alone. She's strong Robert. I'm sure they're okay. The phone probably died or something. You know how crappy those things are. Or maybe, well you know how she is, maybe she just doesn't want to talk to you right now. I'm sure picking up Brian stirred up some emotions."

"Yeah, you're probably right, Dave. Want a smoke? I've got to give these up by the morning. I can't smoke down there. It clogs up the air filters too quick."

"Sure, I'll take one. Why not, right?"

Dave takes a small drag and coughs. They both laugh. Robert reaches over and takes a sip from the bottle. They both smoke quietly and look at the open night sky, filled with stars.

They go back inside after a few minutes of silence, reflection. Dave and his family go to sleep in one of the bedrooms. Robert lies down on the couch where Mr. Roark once slept, and died.

Robert closes his eyes to sleep but his mind races with memories of his entire life, all of the decisions that led to this point in time, the good and the bad. He sees the light blue dawn, slowly beginning to creep through the window beside him. He begins to doubt that Julia will come. Maybe she would take her chances with Brian and Justin, and go into hiding with one of his contacts she met on the road. She probably found a nicer place, that didn't involve going underground.

He doubts his decision on ever putting her in the bunker the first time. He hopes that she made the comment about not going back to the bunker out of anger that day. But now, he thinks maybe she really meant it.

Robert's thoughts are interrupted. Reports of AGI facility explosions start broadcasting on his transistor radio and continue throughout the night. At least they weren't going down without some type of a fight, he thinks to himself. He takes notes of the facility locations and plots them on the map.

The darkness slowly fades away, along with his belief of ever seeing Julia again.

* * *

Robert lights another cigarette, still unable to sleep.

Then, out of the silence he hears a light cracking of wood, close to the side of the cabin.

He slowly clicks off the safety of a handgun and takes aim at the back door.

There's a light series of footsteps on the stairs and three figures appear at the door.

Robert sits up.

It was them. She had come back. He couldn't believe it.

He stands and places the gun on safe, putting it down.

Julia and Robert lock eyes through the window and across the low-lit cabin. He begins walking toward the back door. Julia can see the emotion in his eyes as he walks toward her.

Robert was happy to see Justin and Brian standing there as well, but seeing Julia resuscitated new life into him.

Without realizing it and without controlling his body, he was now right in front of her, wrapping her tightly in his arms.

Julia feels his arms wrap tightly around her.

She had not felt his touch for so long, but then instantly, a remembered sense of warmth, safety, and love, came rushing back though her body. She thought she didn't back away at first because she was exhausted, and just wasn't thinking clearly. But now, as she found her arms tightly wrapped around him without realizing what she had done, or without controlling her body, she knew that this was right.

Julia knew then, in that moment, that she had made the right decision to follow her road less travelled, forgiveness.

The moment is brief, but it feels like an eternity, for both of them.

* * *

They separate.

Robert hugs Justin as well. Brian backs away at his attempt. Robert sees the zip ties and Julia explains.

Dave and Amy come out to the noises and they all talk excitedly about their own journeys that got them all there. Their conversations dwindle down and begin to circle around each other.

They all start packing up after their brief reunion. Then they sanitize the cabin and begin walking towards the bunker, and the remaining conversations quickly fade away.

They all begin thinking about their new way of life that soon awaited them, and how everything they had known would never be the same again.

FORTY-TWO

Robert helps them down the hatch, one by one. He takes one step in after everyone is down at the bottom. He looks down and sees them all huddled around the small circle of sunlight, beaming down the hatch. They are all looking back up at him, and at the sky. He looks up one last time at the sun, the sky, and the trees, and then he closes the hatch. He seals the hatch from the inside, along with the subsequent hatches, sealing them all in, together.

* * *

Julia now found herself once again in the same bunker, the same bunker she thought she would die in over a year ago, alone and forgotten. Julia looks around at everyone, and then she looks at her father. She sees him looking at her, deeply, with love, the love that only a father can give. And Julia smiles. Because just then, in that moment, with her father looking back at her, Julia realizes that she was never alone, she was never forgotten.

Thank You

I would personally like to thank you for reading my debut novel, American Z.

And most of all, and most importantly, I hope you enjoyed it.

Sincerely, J.G. Fletcher

About the Author

J.G. Fletcher is a self-published, American author of fiction. He is a resident of Clarksville, TN and alumnus of Austin Peay State University, TN. He graduated with honors from APSU, with a BS in Criminal Justice/Homeland Security and a MS in Management.

J.G. Fletcher has also been serving proudly in the Armed Forces since 2001. He is a Veteran of Operation Iraqi Freedom and Operation Enduring Freedom.

Other Published Works

American Z Bloodlinez

TSOMBIE

Join the TSOMBIE Program today and receive your Phase Three Message Package, which includes newsletters and promotional discounts. More information about this and the author, including current and future works, can be found on the official author websites listed below.

Official Website:
https://jg-fletcher.com   or   https://tsombie.com

Facebook Page:
https://www.facebook.com/AmericanZOfficialBook

Author Email:
jg-fletcher@jg-fletcher.com

www.ingramcontent.com/pod-product-compliance
Lightning Source LLC
Chambersburg PA
CBHW070838250626
47159CB00003B/830